MAX'S CAMPERVAN CASE FILES BOOK 8

VEILED THREATS AND Upset Pets

TYLER RHODES

Copyright © 2024 Tyler Rhodes

All rights reserved. This book or any portion thereof may not be reproduced or used in any manner whatsoever without the express written permission of the author except for the use of brief quotations in a book review.

This is a work of fiction. Names, characters, businesses, places, events and incidents are either the products of the author's imagination or used in a fictitious manner. Any resemblance to actual persons, living or dead, or actual events is purely coincidental.

Dedicated to everyone with a spare sleeping bag for camping.
Yes, we've all spilt wine at least once!

Chapter 1

Light bounced off the estuary feeding into the Bristol Channel as we crossed the Severn bridge early on Saturday morning. We made good progress, as more people were heading out of Wales and into England towards Bristol than vice versa.

The day was as bright as our spirits as my faithful companion and I hummed and howled along to an eighties mixtape I'd uncovered sorting through my things in the attic when Min and I divorced and I left our home for good.

Nena's *99 Red Balloons* morphed into *Kids in America* by Kim Wilde, who, by all accounts, was now a garden designer. Soon enough, we sailed past the signs for Newport, with Cardiff a mere twenty minutes away if the M4 flowed well.

I stifled a yawn, then smiled. It had been a very early start, but we'd ended up staying at such a lovely spot for a week that neither Anxious nor I wanted to leave, so we would now arrive the morning of Uncle Ernie's wedding. He was a bag of nerves when I'd called him yesterday, but said that he, too, wouldn't be at St Davids until late morning. There was so much to organise, and the actual wedding was being taken care of by his wife-to-be and her sister. Uncle Ernie had hinted that they were professional wedding planners with a difference, but refused to elaborate.

I was still amazed he was getting married after only knowing someone for a few weeks, but once again he insisted she was the one for him, and that being in his fifties meant he didn't have time to hang around. After a rather cryptic conversation where he said the wedding would take hours, I was left with more questions than answers but wouldn't have expected anything less from him.

The utter ska nut had gone down a storm at Lydstock when his band, The Skankin' Skeletons, had headlined on day one. Music was his life, and I assumed today's wedding would be a unique and raucous affair. Most likely, it would be ska themed, as I couldn't imagine him marrying anyone that didn't love the upbeat music style as much as him.

I shook my head and smiled as I pictured a wild party with ska and punk dominating the sound system, and could only wonder at what the actual wedding would be like. Unconventional, for sure.

Jump Around by House of Pain accompanied us as we passed the turn for Cardiff, then before I knew it we were approaching Bridgend, a once thriving mining town like so many in this part of South Wales that had fallen into sharp decline once the mines closed and the work dried up almost overnight. Buildings made of dark local stone did little to lighten the brooding atmosphere as the old slag heaps of Port Talbot and the sprawling mess of the steelworks cast a dark stain on an otherwise lush landscape, the looming hills dotted with sheep on sharp inclines always making me worry there would be a sheep avalanche.

We soon closed in on Swansea, the last major town for miles, and the mixtape was replaced with one of Uncle Ernie's cassettes to keep us in the right mood for what was, after all, a day of celebration. When he'd given me the tape at Lydstock, I'd been surprised, but he explained that most bands had reverted to making LPs and cassettes now as the younger generation had become interested in formats that had basically died out with the advent of CDs and the digital revolution. I'd never been a big user of streaming services, though, and now I was a man of no fixed abode and often dodgy internet signal I had no intention of starting.

The M4 motorway trailed off and we were now back to narrower roads for the rest of the trip. Wales was big on small, windy roads, and unmanned roadworks signs and temporary traffic lights seemed to be a national pastime, so the going would be much slower as we approached the most westerly point of West Wales. The further we got, the lower our speed, but it gave us time to enjoy the increasingly stunning scenery as we wove around hills, traversed rugged mountains, and became lost in dense thickets of trees before emerging into blinding sunlight as we bypassed Haverfordwest and suddenly found ourselves hugging the road right by the coast and got our first glimpse of the sea.

"That's St. Bride's Bay, Anxious." I pointed out of his window where he'd been sitting up and admiring the view for the last half hour since having a doze.

Anxious turned, his ears sprang to attention, and his tail swished across the faded upholstery of my beloved VW campervan. He yipped excitedly then locked his intense gaze on me, the question clear.

"Yes," I chuckled, "we can go for a walk on the beach there if you like? And don't forget I promised we'd go fishing. I have my gear in the back, and we haven't had a chance to use it yet. You can't beat fresh fish. We'll find a campsite later on, closer to St Davids but right by the water, and we can have a fun few days exploring. This is an incredibly beautiful part of Wales, with lots of beaches, endless walks in the country, and there are even islands you can visit."

Anxious barked, then looked out to sea.

"No, I don't think we'll go island hopping, but we'll certainly hit a few beaches and take our time enjoying the area. But first we have to get to St Davids and maybe have a look at the cathedral. There's a medieval building opposite, called the Bishop's Palace if I recall correctly, which is a ruin but really stunning. This is actually the smallest city in Britain by population. Only a thousand or so residents, but it's popular with tourists."

Anxious barked another question, so I played along and answered like we were having a normal conversation. Sometimes I wondered if we were really this in-tune, or I just wanted him to be able to talk so made the rest up. In the end, I decided it didn't matter.

"Why, you ask? Because of the beaches, the clean water for swimming, the scenery, the lovely cathedral, and the fact it's away from everything and nice and quiet. The roads may be narrow, but it doesn't get congested like in Cornwall, so has become more popular every year. There are scores of ancient monuments, and it's also a pilgrimage destination which has been going on for centuries."

Anxious may have lost interest in the details, but he smiled anyway then continued to stare out of the window. Glimpses of white sand and steep cliffs teased us before we turned away from the coast and glided along for a while before hitting the ubiquitous traffic lights, the road signs in both Welsh and English mocking impatient holidaymakers as there wasn't a workman or a hole in sight.

We got going soon enough, caught sight of the coast again, then headed straight towards St Davids for the final leg of our enjoyable but long trip. Vee hummed nicely, the ride smooth and enjoyable even on less than ideal roads. Maybe I was just used to the very basic suspension now, or maybe she had warmed to me and Anxious so was performing at her best.

I patted the steering wheel and said a silent thank you just in case she truly did feel like part of the family. My thoughts inevitably drifted to Min the moment the subject of family surfaced. We'd spoken yesterday before she headed off on a well-deserved vacation for a week of sun in foreign climes, so I hoped it was going well.

She'd admitted to being reticent about going away alone, and worried she'd feel strange staying in a hotel with nobody to spend time with, but was also determined to prove to herself that she could do such things. A confidence booster. I was proud of her, and certain she'd make friends and have a wonderful holiday. Not that I didn't wish she was here with us, as I did with all my heart, but there was no rush. Barring me doing something truly idiotic, this time next year we would be back together again, and for life.

With my thoughts elsewhere, I was shocked to discover that we'd basically made it to St Davids. Anxious' ears pricked up as we hit traffic on the main road, noting the people browsing in shop windows, enjoying breakfast at outside cafes, sipping coffees, staring at maps, or just walking and taking in the sights. It was a bustling Saturday morning with tourists out in force in this otherwise sleepy city dominated by the cathedral that historically was what allowed it to have city status rather than what it truly was—a small town hugging the edge of West Wales.

I concentrated on the road signs and navigated the one-way system, then pulled into a car park Uncle Ernie had recommended because it was close to the cathedral and the Bishop's Palace opposite on the other side of the river.

"Blimey, look at this place. I don't know if we'll find a parking spot. I know it's summer and Saturday, but it's still early. Why are so many people here already?"

Anxious glanced from me to the rows of vehicles but had no insight, which was fair enough.

After three circuits of the car park, I was beginning to lose hope and contemplating trying another one, but a Land Rover chugged out of a generous space at the end of a row so I indicated, then pulled alongside the spot before reversing into place in one smooth turn.

"Nice, eh?" I asked, holding up my hand and getting a high-five from my best buddy. "I've been practising, and now it'll be easy to leave later when we go to find somewhere to stay. Maybe we'll camp by Whitesands. It's one of the best beaches in the country, and surfers love it."

Anxious yipped excitedly, so it was settled.

"Okay, it's only ten thirty, so we have ages until the wedding. It starts at two, so we can have a mooch about then get ready. We'll have to find Uncle Ernie later, but he won't be here until midday, so we have hours to relax first."

Anxious was keening to get the day of fun and festivities started, so I grabbed a few things from the back then we headed towards the cathedral and hit the tightly mowed grass within minutes. We were in our element here, out in nature, surrounded by smiling, happy people on vacation with time on their side. No need to rush. Everyone had the whole day ahead of them. No work, just leisurely walks soaking up the atmosphere and history of the twelfth-century cathedral still standing after so many years. A true monument to the skills of those long deceased.

Rather than go inside, we sat on the grassy bank and relaxed. I stretched my legs out while Anxious rested his head in my lap, and before long he was snoring happily.

As I watched folks come and go, I realised what was so special about my new life. It had been like one extended vacation where I got to see everyone at their best. People were on holiday at campsites or places of interest. They were relaxed, taking a break from busy schedules or hectic jobs to unwind and enjoy themselves. The same at festivals. It was infectious, and lifted my spirits, but I couldn't help looking forward to later in the year.

Instead of busy campsites or crowds of holidaymakers, I'd have a more isolated, lonely existence, and the weather would be a real issue. So far, it had been one gloriously sunny day after another, with the rest of the summer still ahead of me. The unprecedented heatwave had left the country gasping and confused, but I loved it! What would it be like when it was cold and wet and I couldn't hang a tea towel out to dry, let alone sit out in shorts and a vest, my Crocs beside me on the grass?

I guess I'd find out, and was relishing the challenge. The change would do me good. A real test of a new way of life I was determined to stick to. I would never go back to conventional living as long as Min decided to join me in Vee, my adorable 67 VW.

But right now, I was content to enjoy the present. Sitting on a grass bank with my dog in my lap, watching tourists, and marvelling at a building almost a thousand years old and still going strong.

The longer I sat, the more I realised there were a truly astonishing number of people with dogs today. At places like this, there were always more than your fair share of pets as owners often chose the UK to holiday in so they could bring their dogs with them, but almost every other person here seemed to have one. And not just regular dogs, but very well-groomed animals. Poodles were in abundance, their curly coats immaculate, and several sported fancy bows.

Chihuahuas trotted alongside couples, smartly dressed men carried Pomeranians in their arms like babes, sprightly Springer Spaniels bounced around smiling couples, one eye on them, the other on the lookout for a ball. On and on it went. A constant stream of dogs and people, and they all seemed to be heading towards the ruins of the Bishop's Palace across the river.

As the parade continued, Anxious began to kick and whimper in his sleep, until his keen sense of smell clearly roused him from his slumber. He bounced off my lap, sat up, snorted several times, and began to wag happily as he watched the procession go by.

"It's a busy day for dogs," I noted. "Uncle Ernie hasn't been very forthcoming with what's going on today. Let's check it out, and see if we can find him and get to the bottom of this."

Already on his feet, Anxious waited while I stood, then cocked his head, asking if he could go and play. I explained that this wasn't the place to be tearing around, so he remained by my side, only stopping occasionally for a sniff as we joined the path and headed to the other side of the river.

Barks and howls, yips and grunts, shouts of "Sit," and the endless call of dog names grew in intensity the closer we got, until we finally arrived in the grounds of the ruins amidst what could best be described as barely controlled chaos.

Dogs were everywhere, and Anxious darted from my side and began tearing around with a playful Lab before others joined them and a small gang of excited pooches raced around the paths, startling people who clearly hadn't expected such a commotion when they came to investigate the expansive ruins.

Decorative bunting and an awful lot of flowers were arranged at one side of the building where a large table had been set up to register guests. I read the sign with a sinking heart, wondering what on earth Uncle Ernie had been thinking.

"Dog Wedding Day," I read aloud, astonished. I'd heard of dogs getting married, but never thought it was an actual real thing, especially a group thing, but the more I overheard, and the longer I remained amidst the chaos, the more evident it was that, yes, this was indeed a day where people could bring their dogs and get them hitched.

And Uncle Ernie was going to get married here soon? Could that be true?

"Max, you made it!"

I jumped in shock, then turned to see my uncle smiling broadly at me. "I sure did. And so did about every dog in Wales by the looks of it. Uncle Ernie, what's going on?"

"Sorry I didn't tell you," he said sheepishly with a wink and smile, "but I thought it would be a fun surprise. I've got my smartest gear on and I'm good to go, but there are a few hours yet. Time for some lunch, then the wedding, and later an awesome party!"

"You do look great. New braces?" I asked, still unable to believe what I was seeing and hearing.

He pulled then released his braces, the blood-red elastic snapping against a pristine white Fred Perry polo shirt, his black drainpipe trousers hitched high as always to show off white socks and shiny black shoes, his usual ska-inspired dress code but clearly brand new for his big day. He lifted his trilby and brushed at a fresh buzzcut before replacing it and winking a glinting blue eye at me.

"I bought the best clobber I could afford for the big day," he grinned.

"You're very tanned too. Been getting some sun?"

"Got to look my best for my special lady. Ah, there she is. What a looker, eh? She's such a sweetheart."

I watched a slim woman dressed almost identically to my uncle chatting to a group of people, and she waved when she looked our way. Uncle Ernie beamed as he waved back happily. She hurried off as if she'd forgotten something important, lost to the dense crowd.

"She's mad busy at the moment, but I'll introduce you to her soon. Max, thanks so much for coming. I know this seems weird, but my Freya is really into the whole thing as it's the business she runs with her sister, so don't say anything rude, okay? I know it's odd, but I love her and this is just a bit of fun."

"Of course. It's fine. Let's go say hello when she comes back. I'm sure it's—"

"Help. Somebody help him!"

We turned to see a woman pointing up at the remains of the Bishop's Palace. A man stood on the ancient ruined wall above a circular window. He shielded his eyes from the sun, making it appear like he saluted, then leaned forward. Everyone gasped, and then he simply fell from the building and landed with a thud on the ground below.

People rushed forward, shouting for help, asking if there was a doctor present, but I knew he would have died instantly from such a height.

"Here we go again," I said sadly as Uncle Ernie gripped my shoulder and the dogs went wild.

Chapter 2

Freya rushed over to us in a flood of tears and asked Uncle Ernie, "Was that Neil? It can't be, can it?"

"I'm sorry, love, but it was. I don't know how to tell you this, but he jumped."

"Don't talk rubbish," she screamed, tugging at a plaited pigtail, her tanned face darkening as beads of sweat sprang to the surface, her heavy eye makeup beginning to run. She wiped at quivering lips, smearing bright red lipstick. "My brother-in-law would never do that."

"I'm so sorry," I said, knowing it was lame, but what else could I say?

"Thank you. I need to see."

"We'll come, but don't get too close," warned Uncle Ernie. He took Freya's hand and we hurried along with everyone else to the base of the wall.

Freya dragged him through the crowd of people and dogs while Anxious and I followed close behind, the noise levels deafening as everyone shouted or sobbed and the animals barked and whined.

We emerged into empty ground, the guests keeping their distance apart from a woman wearing clothes identical to Uncle Ernie and Freya.

"Susie, was it really him? Was it Neil?"

The crouched woman turned, her long dark hair hanging over her face. She tugged it back, revealing a steady stream of tears, her makeup, like Freya's, utterly ruined. "He's dead, Freya. Neil's dead."

Freya rushed forward and knelt beside the woman and they hugged tight.

"Susie is Freya's sister, and that poor man is Susie's husband," explained Uncle Ernie. He put his mouth right next to my ear and whispered, "Neil wasn't a nice guy. Unkind, mean, and a bully."

"And he jumped off a ruin on the day of his sister-in-law's wedding? Was he having problems?"

"Not that I know of. Max, sorry about this, but it seems like there's another dead body."

"Yes, and that's awful, but at least it wasn't murder. What drives someone to kill themselves like that?"

"Dunno, and to be honest, nephew, I'm finding it hard to believe. Neil might not have been the jolliest of guys, but this is way out of character. Come on, let's give them a hand."

We bent beside the sisters, who still held each other tight. Neil was clearly deceased, the wounds extreme, but already the sirens of an ambulance could be heard, and no doubt it would be confirmed by the professionals soon enough. Regardless, Uncle Ernie checked for signs of life then shook his head. Susie sobbed into Freya's shoulder.

"We're all so sorry," said Uncle Ernie when Susie shifted back and sat beside her husband.

"We are," I agreed. "I'm Max, Ernie's nephew."

"Nice to meet you, Max," said Freya, smiling weakly.

"Hello. I've heard a lot about you," mumbled Susie, her words almost slurred because of the shock.

"Let's get you away from here," Freya told Susie. She nodded to Uncle Ernie, and together they helped an unprotesting Susie to stand.

She was numb with shock, her arms pinned to her sides, all three dressed identically. The sisters had matching figures. Slim, almost skinny like Uncle Ernie, with tanned faces and arms. Whereas Uncle Ernie had what you would call a lived-in face, the sisters were smooth of complexion and probably in their early fifties like him, although I got the feeling that Susie was a few years younger than Freya. The difference was the hair. Freya's was blond from a bottle, but a good dye job and in cute plaited pigtails, whereas Susie's was straight, dyed jet black, and hung loose.

"Where's my darling boy?" asked Freya in a panic. She scanned the crowd, eyes widening, then sighed and relaxed her shoulders as Anxious and the boisterous Lab came charging into the empty space past people gawping and discussing the terrible events. "There you are," she chastised as the dogs sat in front of us.

"Anxious, have you been playing with your new friend?" I asked.

He barked a yes, and the Lab joined him. Both were panting heavily. Suddenly, the Lab stiffened, and his tail lowered as he sniffed. Taking his cue from his new buddy, Anxious sniffed, too, then they both tracked over to Neil.

"That's Freya's dog, Special," said Uncle Ernie, filling me in on more information. "He's getting married today to a fine Lab called Two-tone."

"I assume he's called Special as he's named after The Specials, and Two-tone is the dog of a ska lover?" I asked, raising an eyebrow.

"How did you guess?" he chortled, then glanced at the women and shook his head in apology.

"Special, come here, boy," Freya called, but the pair were already racing towards the wall then ran through the opening into the ruin's interior.

"I'll go and get them," I said. "Again, I'm so sorry."

"Who could have killed my poor husband?" wailed Susie, clutching at Freya as though she had answers.

My uncle and I exchanged a confused look, then he put a hand to Susie's shoulder and said, "Nobody killed him, Susie. We saw him jump."

Susie's head shot up and she snapped, "Don't be ridiculous! Why would he jump? He doesn't even like heights. What was he doing up there?"

"We both saw him lean forward, then he fell," I explained. "It was a terrible thing, but it happened."

"No. I refuse to believe that. Max, I know about you, as Ernie never stops singing your praises, so I want you to help me. Please? You must. Somebody killed my Neil and I want you to uncover who."

"Let me go and get the dogs, and I'll speak to you later, but I think you should sit down somewhere."

"I'm staying right here until the ambulance arrives." Susie stomped her foot and crossed her arms. She was clearly a determined woman who took no nonsense. Just like her sister, I assumed.

"Okay, I understand." I hurried after Anxious and his new friend, Special, my senses attuned for anything untoward now Susie was certain this was no suicide. Reliving the event of a few minutes past, I tried to recall if anything was wrong, but all I could remember was seeing Neil on top of the wall, shielding his eyes, then leaning forward and falling. There wasn't anyone else there. Nobody had pushed him, and nobody had come rushing down from the wall as surely they would have been seen?

But that wasn't quite true. If someone had been up there with him, they could have easily hidden behind the wall and exited the building in any number of ways then blended in. Nobody would have been any the wiser.

I spotted Anxious and Special, but took my time approaching as I studied the ancient wall for anything strange. It was very impressive, and easily ten metres high, with several round windows with carved surrounds in fine condition. The top still retained the original shape of the roof gone long ago, but sections, like where Neil had fallen, were flattened off and I assumed fortified to stop the entire structure crumbling.

I got a sense of the scale of the home for the bishop of the time, the building enlarged to accommodate his living quarters and a massive area for banqueting and impressing visitors. St Davids was a mecca for pilgrims many years ago, with the pope having declared that two visits to St Davids equated to a single pilgrimage to Rome, so it was known throughout the world.

The grass was kept short, the interior pristine to showcase the fine medieval architecture. The dogs had no interest in such things, but were sniffing around by the wall. Anxious took his lead from Special, who clearly knew the scent of Neil, so both were right up by the wall and on their hind legs.

Looking up, I noted that it would be relatively easy to climb up from this side, the stone more eroded, the thick walls now almost like steps where they'd fallen away over time but solidified with mortar to keep the structure sound. It was a steep climb, for sure, and no easy undertaking, but it was doable, which was rather a duh moment as obviously it was because Neil had got right to the top.

"Can you track who was here?" I asked Anxious, then squatted and said, "Hello, Special. I'm Max, a relative of Ernie's. He's marrying Freya, your owner. Do you like Uncle Ernie?"

Special barked in the affirmative, and I laughed, then ruffled his back. Anxious came in for a fuss, too, so I petted them both before standing and asking again, "Can you track who was here?"

Special sniffed the ground, then raced back to Neil, but I called for him and he returned. "No, the other person. Was there somebody else here?"

Anxious sat, tail wagging, eyes glued on my pocket. Special somehow sensed that there was a treat to be had if he played his cards right, and sat beside Anxious; both began to drool.

"Fine, a biscuit each if you discover who was here. Not that man, but someone else?" I pointed to Neil, shook my head, then pulled out two biscuits. "Find the stranger."

The dogs got to work immediately, and returned to the wall, sniffed, then tracked back and forth, gradually going deeper into the grounds before leaving through a doorway halfway along the right-hand side wall. I followed, keeping my distance so I didn't disturb them, but the moment I exited I knew it was a lost cause. People and animals were everywhere and the dogs were sitting on the grass, panting happily. No prizes for guessing where their focus was.

"Well done, and it was worth a try." I gave them both their treat and they laid down and happily munched on their snacks before Special raced back to Freya and Anxious joined me.

"It looks like we might be involved in another murder mystery," I explained. "I'm not sure anything went on here apart from the obvious, but keep your ears open and your nose primed." Anxious barked that he would do just that, so we returned to the others as I scanned the various groups but noted nothing suspicious beyond a lot of very weird people and animals.

The snippets of conversation I overheard consisted of three subjects. The apparent suicide, Uncle Ernie and Freya's wedding, and the weddings of the dogs. I estimated a few hundred people were gathered, and wondered exactly how many dogs were to be wed today. How long would it take? Would it even go ahead now? Everyone was concerned, and although a man was dead, it was clear that nobody wanted to call this off.

"The ambulance shouldn't be long," I noted as I joined the others, still waiting by Neil.

"Not much use now, are they?" Uncle Ernie shrugged.

"No, but it's how these things work. Maybe we should take a seat?" I suggested, indicating poor Susie who was in a terrible state and constantly tugging at her wedding ring and glancing at Neil as if he might somehow jump up and declare that he was fine.

"I can't leave him. Not yet. Who would do this to him? He was such a kind man. A great husband and such a considerate person."

Uncle Ernie snorted, and I glanced at him, but he covered it up with a cough and nobody else noticed. He caught my look but shook his head; now was not the time.

"It wasn't murder, honey," soothed Freya, hugging her sister. "Everyone saw it. I know it's hard, but he jumped."

"Never! Stop saying that!"

"Sorry. I didn't mean to upset you."

"It's okay. This is just such a shock." Susie turned and shouted, "Why are you gawping? Get about your business. There's a wedding to plan and everyone make sure their pets are ready and know what to do. You people need to go and practice with your animals. And if I find even a whiff of dog poo anywhere, there will be trouble."

People murmured their apologies and offered their condolences for her loss, but there were plenty of smiles too. They wanted this event to go ahead and were relieved that it seemed like it would.

"You can't be serious?" said Freya. "Susie, Neil's dead. We can't have our wedding and the others. It wouldn't be right."

"You know Neil was always very down on our business, but we pulled it off anyway. Look how far we've come. We can't cancel. It will ruin us. Top Dog Weddings will not go bust because of this." Susie dabbed at her eyes with a tissue, then wiped her nose and stared at the scrunched paper like it had answers. "Gosh, it's stained black and red. My makeup must be as bad as yours. Is it?"

"It's all run, yes, and I don't think I want to know what I look like." Nevertheless, Freya pulled a compact from her bag and checked herself over, tutting while she cleaned her face.

"Why don't you two ladies go and sort out your faces?" suggested Uncle Ernie. "It will help you feel better. I know that sounds dumb, but it might give you something to focus on."

"Yes, good idea, love." Freya beamed at him, then took her sister off to a bank where they sat and could still see Neil, but at least they had some space.

"Max," whispered Uncle Ernie, pulling me off to one side.

"What is it?"

"Neil was not the best husband in the world like Susie would have you believe. They had real issues. Susie wasn't happy, and he had an affair last year. He's a very well-known corporate type, made tons of cash helping companies close down small businesses so they could eliminate the competition, and it hit the papers. Nearly tore them apart. They've been trying to fix their marriage, but from what I hear via Freya, it wasn't going so well."

"So he wasn't in a good place?"

"I don't know. Freya only told me what Susie shared with her, which was mostly about how she was feeling. Seems like Neil was trying to make things right, but I don't know if he was depressed. There was certainly nothing mentioned about him being suicidal. That's a whole other ball game."

"So what do you reckon? Would he jump, or is Susie right and this was murder?"

"I think we need to figure out exactly what happened here, and that begins with sorting out how the fool got up there in the first place. You took a look. What did you see?"

"Maybe it's best we both check it out?"

He agreed, so we entered through the gable end of the east wing and into the Great Hall.

"Wow, what incredible workmanship," gasped Uncle Ernie, always a fan of ancient architecture. "They're called arcaded parapets because of the arches. You can walk around a lot of it, even now, after the repairs that have been done."

"But there's no parapet leading directly to the gable wall."

"No, but look, he could have easily climbed up over there, walked along the top of the wall, then jumped."

"He could," I admitted, noting the relatively easy access again from various points, "but why go to the trouble? And if you're hellbent on killing yourself, you'd be a nervous wreck and hardly able to climb and keep your balance."

"I know I would be. Let's get up there and investigate."

"You've got your wedding outfit on. And I'm in Crocs and shorts."

"So we better hurry. You need to get changed into something smart for my big day." He winked, then pulled me in for a hug.

"I've got clothes in the camper."

"Don't worry about that. I told you to leave it to me. I have an outfit just like mine. You'll look great."

"You think? I'm not really a ska style kind of guy. More hippy than two-tone."

"But you'll wear it for me and Freya? We want everyone to match."

"Sure. Of course."

We searched until we found the best way up, which turned out to be a proper set of stairs, and emerged onto the arcaded parapet. After some tricky manoeuvring, we found ourselves on a newly refurbished and thankfully very solid floor directly behind the wheel window. The carved surrounds were as impressive as everything else, and the tiny opening beneath it afforded a dizzying view of the ground far below.

"I didn't even know this was here," said Uncle Ernie, beaming. "How cool is this? You can see over the side walls and through the parapet, but it's the carved window that's the most impressive."

"It's incredible, but why clamber up when he could have hopped onto the lower parapet and jumped?"

"Because everyone was gathered around the other side. And it would be easy. See."

Before I could stop him, Uncle Ernie vaulted onto the parapet then over and began to ascend the gable wall.

"Uncle Ernie, I get it. Please come down. Freya will kill me if you die," I joked, my heart lurching.

"Sure, but I'm fine. I'm like a monkey."

"Hairy and with big teeth," I teased, relieved when he hopped down.

"And still clean." He indicated his spotless outfit, and I laughed with relief.

We heard a commotion from below, so peered over the side to discover the paramedics and police had arrived.

"We better go down," said Uncle Ernie.

"We should." I did a quick circuit of the parapet, and discovered an empty bottle of water, a child's red glove, an empty pack of Walker's crisps, cheese and onion as they're the best, and nestled right in a corner, a ring with an impressive diamond.

"Check this out," I called, beckoning my uncle over.

"A wedding ring?"

"No, an engagement ring. You just do plain rings for weddings. And you do have yours, don't you?"

"Of course. No way will I lose it. I'll give it to you later, just so I know it's safe, but what does this mean?"

We both peered at the ring as it glinted in the sunshine. Heat radiated from the floor and walls, and I began to sweat.

"I have no idea. Either someone got turned down after proposing and left the ring behind, it got lost, or this has something to do with why Neil went over the wall."

"Then we have a real mystery on our hands." Uncle Ernie turned and smiled at me. "Now all we need to discover is if it's a suicide mystery, or a murder mystery."

Chapter 3

I snapped a few photos, and even though it felt silly to photograph a water bottle and packet of crisps as well as the ring and glove, I did it anyway. By the time we descended, the place was swarming with the authorities. Even the fire service was here, I assumed to ensure the police could get up onto the walls safely.

Neil had already been moved, and I wasn't sure that was right as there was no sign of a detective yet. But the one thing I'd learned after so many murder investigations was that opinions differed regards what to do once a body had been discovered, especially if the paramedics believed the death was an accident, or, in this case, something altogether more upsetting. They had the deceased's loved ones to consider, and as Susie was here they clearly believed it best to put Neil somewhere more dignified.

The area was cordoned off, however, but several keen officers who stood guard and turned people away were bombarded with questions about the chance of the day's planned events going ahead. That was the main concern now, it seemed, and I didn't begrudge them their rather insensitive remarks. Unless you are directly involved in such things, it's difficult to feel more than sad, but you don't want the death of a stranger to disrupt your own life.

"What happens now?" asked Uncle Ernie, dabbing at his brow with a handkerchief.

"Now we need to get out of the sun before we melt. Susie and Freya are heading over there, so let's catch them up."

"Good idea. They're probably going to the ambulance. Think we need to hang around to answer questions?"

"We'll come back in a while. Let's check on them first."

As more officers strode across the grass towards the scene, I spotted Anxious with his new best buddy, Special, so called and they came charging over, looking utterly worn out by the carnival atmosphere.

"No running off. This is a sad time, so you should be sticking with Freya or us."

Both looked desolate for the time it took to have a quick wag, then we hurried over to the two women now sitting on a grassy bank far enough away to be left alone for a while.

"Who are these people?"

Uncle Ernie grinned as he turned back to look at the chaos behind us, then said, "People who want a fun day out. Freya and Susie started a dog wedding planning business a few years ago and it really took off. Top Dog Weddings is the name. Cool, eh? There are plenty of owners who think it's a fun, sweet thing to do. Lots of dogs have best buddies, and them getting hitched is an excuse for an exciting day."

"Bit strange though, right? It isn't a legal contract."

"No, maybe not, but what it does is bring the owners together and make their friendship closer. It's probably more about the people than the dogs, to be honest."

"And they do well?"

"They do really well. It ain't cheap, which is why they arrange a few of these mass events every year. Neil thought it was utterly ridiculous, and hated the whole idea."

"Why? It's not easy to find a job these days, and if his wife enjoyed it, what's the harm?"

"Exactly. He was just up himself. I didn't like the guy much, but we were always polite to each other." Uncle Ernie glanced away and frowned.

"Come on. Tell the truth."

"Okay, the guy was an utter muppet. Always making snide comments, belittling Susie, laughing at her business. He was the same with me. Said I was past it and should grow up. He'd always make little jabs at everyone. One of those blokes who thought he was better than everyone else. Said I should stop messing around with my music thing and get a real job, although I'd probably only be good for sweeping roads or working in a supermarket as I had no qualifications."

"Those are important jobs. I respect anyone that works to put bread on the table."

"Exactly! But not Neil. He was a super-straight, uptight guy who thought everyone should wear a suit and tie and toe the line. Right corporate stiff. The exact opposite of me and Freya, and Susie to some extent. She's not into the music like us, but she's still a free spirit and the two are really close."

"Sounds like this Neil would have hated today."

Uncle Ernie laughed. "Absolutely, he did. I'm amazed he came. He was grumbling the moment I saw him earlier. The fool refused to wear the clothes Susie had got him, and kept his suit and tie on, as if it was beneath him. He didn't even like dogs."

"What!? Everyone loves dogs."

"Not him. He was an idiot, basically."

"But Susie stuck with him even after he played around?" The heat was getting to me and my long brown hair hung limp over my face, so I brushed it back and we paused in the shade of a tree for a moment to finish our conversation.

"It's complicated. That's how life is. Money was involved, like always, and she wanted to forgive him and make it work. Max, she was clinging to something that was already over. It's not like with you and Min. There was no real love. Just him being a bully and more than happy to have a wife to make it easier climbing the corporate ladder. Parties and whatnot. The usual boring stuff guys like them spend their time doing to get a raise and make their lives and everyone else's more miserable."

"Wow, that's a bit judgemental. Not everyone with a good job is like that."

"Maybe it is, but I say it how I see it. He was bad news. He made a living closing down businesses in any way he could. Always looking for an angle so his clients could profit from other people's misery. Not cool."

"So there are a fair few people who wouldn't mind shoving him off a high wall?"

"Most of the people who knew him, I'd imagine."

"Where do we start looking into things?"

"Right here. He's probably insulted half the guests and all the dogs. Susie wanted him to come, to try to get him to loosen up and see what a fun event it is, but Freya wasn't happy about it."

"Did they have words?"

"Max, I know you're doing your thing and trying to figure this out, but I'll tell you now, there's no way Freya was involved. Or Susie for that matter."

"Just trying to get a clear picture of the relationships," I said, putting my arms out, palms up, and shrugging.

"I know, and you're a good lad." Uncle Ernie patted my shoulder and smiled; he looked exhausted. "But so you know, they didn't have words. Freya went along with Neil being here as he was her sister's husband. We just want to get married and be happy."

"And we haven't even got to the part about how come you're getting married so suddenly. Freya seems lovely, but it's very rushed."

"I've seen her around at gigs for almost a year now, and we always chatted. Then I got to thinking maybe she was coming to see me, not the band, so I asked her outright."

"You always were blunt."

"That's my style," he grinned. "She admitted she liked me, so we went out, and it moved pretty quickly. You know I've been single for years ever since… Anyway, I don't want to dwell on the past. She's to be my second wife, and I won't let this one get taken by the cancer, God bless my poor wife's soul. I think I deserve to be happy."

"Of course you do. Absolutely."

"Thanks. Freya was married, too, but divorced, with one adult son. He's in Australia and couldn't make it, but she feels the same as me. If we know this is right, why mess around? We're in our fifties, so we're going for it while we still can."

"Then good for you."

We hugged, then dashed across the open ground, the angry sun evaporating what little moisture there was, leaving us gasping, and settled beside the others. Anxious scooted over on his belly and ninja-slid onto my lap, his body like a hot water bottle, making my thighs sweat and my temperature soar.

"He's so adorable," sighed Susie as she stroked his head.

Not to be outdone, the much larger Special flopped upside down over Susie's shins, opened his legs, and barked.

Susie laughed, and it was nice to see her have this brief moment of happiness. It was short-lived, though, and her smile faded as her eyes welled.

"Special is very cute too. He's getting married today?"

"Yes. Do you think Anxious would like to get married too?" Susie smiled wanly, but it was clear her thoughts were elsewhere.

"He's content with me and Min. That's my ex-wife."

"I heard about your divorce from Ernie. I hope that's okay?"

"I didn't go into details, just that you were a changed man since it happened, and that my fingers are crossed you guys make it the second time around," he explained, looking uncomfortable.

"It's fine. I don't mind family knowing. Yes, we will make it. As for Anxious getting married, he has two best friends already. Me and Min. We travel a lot, so I don't think that's the best way to start a marriage."

"That's very diplomatic," said Freya with a staccato laugh. "And we haven't even been introduced properly. How terrible. Ernie, do the honours please?"

"My pleasure."

Once we'd said hello in a rather awkward way, we chatted about my trip and theirs and the various issues they'd already faced getting permission for the event. After endless paperwork, they secured two hours and no more this afternoon to have the weddings and clear everything away. As the conversation petered out, our attention turned to the three approaching policemen. Nobody had spoken to the law yet, but now the time had come.

After the officers introduced themselves and gave their condolences, a woman helped Susie away from the scene so she could speak to her. Others chatted with the rest of us, taking statements and asking a few questions, but it was obvious that nobody thought anything other than an unfortunate suicide had occurred, especially with so many eyewitnesses.

I told them exactly what I had seen, so did Uncle Ernie, and it was over in minutes rather than hours. They left to question guests, but with no detective running the case, it seemed like it was in the hands of the most senior police officers to take statements and then that would be it.

"This is weird," I told Uncle Ernie and Freya once we'd given our statements.

"It sure is," sighed Freya, her face clear now she'd had time to redo her makeup and the initial shock had faded. "Where's the detective and the coroner's office people? What about the other teams that should be here?"

"Should they be here if someone just jumps?" asked Uncle Ernie.

"Yes, they should, and you two found that ring. That's suspicious, and might be a clue."

"But you said he jumped!" protested Uncle Ernie.

"I know I did, because you saw him do it, but that doesn't mean the reason shouldn't be discovered. And besides, I'm not so sure now. Let's face it, Neil was an utter plonker, and I did not like that man, but whether he was pushed or not, there still has to be a reason."

"She's right, Uncle Ernie. This is really odd. I don't think they're meant to move the body, so something's going on here that shouldn't be. Let's go chat with the paramedics. The ambulance is still here, right?"

"Over there." Uncle Ernie pointed, and together with the dogs we approached the paramedics waiting outside the vehicle, faces like thunder, with a policeman standing to one side, clearly being ignored on purpose.

"Love, you better introduce yourself," prompted Uncle Ernie as we approached.

"Good idea. Hi, I'm Freya. The man who died is my brother-in-law. Can I ask why you moved the body? You aren't supposed to, are you? But thank you for getting here so fast."

"You better ask her that," growled a young man with a shaved head, a thick beard, and carrying a little extra weight.

"We both agreed," snapped a woman with a black bob haircut, dark eyes, pale skin, and looking as annoyed as her partner. "And we would have been here faster if you hadn't needed the loo."

"You moved the ambulance. I couldn't find you," he grumbled.

"Sorry, this is very unprofessional of us. We were close by, having our break, but Peter needed the bathroom and when he returned we had the call for the suicide. I'm sorry for your loss, it's a terrible thing, but everyone said they saw the man jump and he was, as you know, dead. The wife seemed upset, so we moved him as it was an open and shut case."

"Now we're getting it in the neck from this guy." The paramedic thumbed in the direction of the officer, who made a point of pretending he didn't notice. "And our boss has already given us what for."

"So it isn't usual to move a body after a suicide?" I asked, sure it wasn't.

"Depends," shrugged the man. I read his name tag, Peter. The woman was Amy.

"Every situation is different. But we took photos, and that should be enough for the detective in charge."

"So there will be an investigation?" I asked.

They exchanged a glance, then Peter almost choked, which turned into a cough, his face reddening. When he'd recovered, he said, "Oh yeah, there will be. And it won't be pretty for anyone involved."

"Peter, that's enough. The poor woman lost her brother-in-law."

"Better to warn them now. Look, we're sorry to cause an upset, but the wife, your sister, was distraught so we decided to move the husband. Neil, wasn't it?"

"Yes," said Freya.

"We figured we'd be kind and put him in the ambulance so your sister got a chance to grieve without seeing him like that. A courtesy. Actually, Amy suggested it. I wasn't sure, but it seemed like the right thing to do."

"You know we've done it before. I don't care what the detectives say. Sometimes the family of the deceased need the chance to breathe, to accept it without seeing the horrid mess the jumpers make. Sorry, that was too graphic."

"We understand. Thank you for being so considerate," said Freya, voice little but a whisper. "Is there an issue with the detective?"

"You're about to find out. And we're about to get a thorough telling off. We hope we did the right thing moving Neil, but now I'm not so sure." Peter rubbed at his bald head, already reddening in the sun.

"We appreciate it."

We turned at the commotion, and watched a powerhouse of a man leaving carnage in his wake as he progressed through the press of officers, onlookers, morbidly curious, and teams of crime scene investigators that had just arrived. He was heading our way, and looked furious.

"Blimey, he's really gonna go ape on us this time," said Peter with a gulp.

"He's a bully, so don't let him intimidate you," said Amy. She stood away from the ambulance, squared her shoulders, crossed her arms, and warned, "Don't let him scare you. He's all bark."

"But with plenty of bite too," muttered Peter, looking much less sure of himself than Amy.

"He looks like a sumo wrestler in an expensive suit," noted Uncle Ernie.

"Bloke's mega rich but still works as a DI," explained Peter. "Dai Davies is the name, and he's got a reputation."

"For being rich?" asked Freya.

"For being a real pain in the proverbial," said Amy. "Don't get on his wrong side if you can help it. We're used to it, but it can be a shock. He's not got a very nice bedside manner, so apologies in advance if you find him upsetting," she told Freya.

"Nobody intimidates me. I've dealt with real hard men in the past."

"Amy. Peter," grunted Dai Davies with a scowl as deep as his stomach was wide.

"Detective Davies," said Amy with a smile that elicited an even deeper scowl and a hiss of annoyance from the DI.

"I believe you have my body inside?" He nodded to the ambulance. "I also believe that you took that damn corpse without my say-so and that you're both utter incompetents!" he roared, his face bright red, blood vessels threatening to pop across his nose and cheeks. Fierce blue eyes flared and locked on Amy, making it obvious they'd had issues in the past.

Amy kept her cool even though her fists bunched. She toyed with her smart haircut before smiling and saying, "It was our call, Dai, and the deceased's wife was understandably upset."

"You don't move a body until I arrive and say you can. You disturbed the scene and messed with my investigation. I'll be having words with your superior."

"He already knows," said Peter glumly.

"Good! Now, was he dead on arrival?"

"Hitting the ground, you mean?" asked Peter with a raised eyebrow.

"On your arrival, you utter fool."

"Yes, he was dead. The fall killed him."

"That's not for you to say. That's for the coroner's office to determine once they perform a postmortem."

"Is that really necessary?" asked Freya. "He died when he landed, so that's what killed him."

"Ma'am, I am the lead detective on this case, and how am I to know he was alive when he fell? He may have already been dead, or something might have happened when he landed. My job is to ensure everything is as it seems and nobody killed the deceased. I also need to ascertain why he jumped, if that's what happened. Until I am satisfied, this case will be treated as a murder."

"See, I told you it was murder," said Freya.

"Who are you people? Why are you here?"

Before we could answer, Anxious planted himself in front of the DI and growled a warning. Special sat with his back to Anxious and barked at the paramedics. Then they both stood, swapped places, and repeated their warnings.

"Excuse me," I said, "would you mind keeping your tone light and your manner friendly? The dogs hate shouting, and you're upsetting not only them, but the sister-in-law of the man inside the ambulance. And by the way, his name is Neil, not 'deceased' like you said, which I'm sure you already know."

DI Dai Davies shook with barely concealed rage as he spun slowly to confront me.

This wouldn't be a case where I got along with the person leading the investigation. Although, I couldn't help wondering if there was anything to investigate.

Chapter 4

"Exactly who might you be, sir?" asked the DI in a tone intended to make me uncomfortable.

I kept my posture rigid, and let my six one and broad shoulders from daily exercise expand a little, even though I knew it was churlish. I just hated how he tried to intimidate everyone and wanted to show that his attitude wasn't scaring me.

"He's my nephew," snapped Uncle Ernie, glaring at the DI. "I'm Ernie, Freya here is my wife-to-be, and we're here for our wedding."

"And a wedding for dogs, so I hear. Utterly ridiculous."

"I think it's super cute," said Amy with a wink at me when I caught her eye.

"Yes, well, that's your opinion," snarled Dai. "Whoever heard of such nonsense?" He focused on Freya and said, "Sorry for your loss. I need to ask you all a few questions. Over here, please."

We trailed after the detective, his sour mood mystifying. Anxious and Special kept pace with him, watching for any sign of aggression, and I knew if he stepped out of line Anxious would be locked onto his ankle quicker than he could snaffle a biscuit.

DI Davies didn't once turn around to check we were following. He merely marched back into the heart of things, his shiny dark blue suit and crisp white shirt cuffs sparkling in the midday sun. For a large man, he moved with an unmistakable confidence and had an easy gait even though some would say he lumbered.

People hopped out of his way before he bowled them over, seeming to sense his approach. Officers especially gave him a wide berth, so he clearly had a reputation in the area.

He sat without speaking at the table set up under a gazebo used earlier by those taking the invitations and registering dogs to be married, currently vacated because of the upset.

"One at a time," he grunted without looking up as he set out his phone, a notepad, and a folder.

"I'll speak to him first," I told Freya softly as she began to shake.

"No, her first." Dai lifted his head and jabbed a thick finger at Freya.

"Mate, you need to cool it with the attitude," warned Uncle Ernie "Elbows" Effort as he put his arm around Freya protectively.

"I am merely doing my job and trying to uncover the truth. If that upsets you, I apologise." He wasn't sorry in the slightest.

"I'll be okay, but don't go far," said Freya, pecking Uncle Ernie on the cheek.

"You sure?"

Freya nodded, then sat opposite the detective just as Susie arrived.

"Susie, are you alright?" asked Freya, jumping up from her seat and rushing to her sister.

"I... yes, I'm fine." She glanced quickly at the detective then burst into tears.

"I assume you've already spoken to Susie?" I asked him.

"I have, and I told you that would be all," he said, staring at her, emotionless.

"Blimey, mate, what is with you?" asked Uncle Ernie, as perplexed by this utter lack of empathy as me.

"Nothing. I just want answers."

Freya and Susie went off to the side for a moment, then returned with Susie more composed. Freya resumed her seat and smiled at us, so we left them to it.

Susie was in her own world and too upset to talk, so we kept her company until Uncle Ernie was called, then I left the sisters alone and waited with Anxious until it was my turn. Dai beckoned me with a crook of his finger, beyond annoying, but I had resolved to remain friendly if only for my own sanity. Getting angry is always a choice, and I chose to be calm and unperturbed. Let him blow a blood vessel; I was going to stay frosty.

"Take a seat," grunted Dai, eyes on his folder. With a sigh, he closed it, then slowly his eyes drifted up to mine.

I smiled.

He scowled.

"So you're Max Effort?"

"I am. The one and only."

"What's your take on this?"

"You want my opinion? I'm surprised."

"I want this solved. You clearly know what you're doing. Why wouldn't I?"

"Because you don't seem the type to want the opinion of the general public."

"I know who you are. You just came from that utter butchery at Chucklefest, and by all accounts from a Detective Dee, you did very well. There are other reports, too, so what's your opinion?"

"It appears to be suicide. I saw him fall. But his wife insists he would never jump, and Freya and Uncle Ernie agree."

"You saying he was pushed?"

"I didn't see anyone. He was in plain sight. He was alone up there."

Dai scribbled in his notebook then fixed his cold blue eyes on me again. "You found the ring the officers retrieved up on the parapet?"

"Yes, and a bottle of water and a crisp packet. Oh, and a glove. Did you go up there?"

"Have you seen the size of me? I can't make it up there. I studied the photos, though, and took a look at the ring. It's expensive. Nobody has reported one missing. That's odd."

"Very," I agreed.

"But to be clear, you witnessed him jump?"

"Not jump as such. He stood there, lifted his hand to shade his eyes, then leaned forward and toppled over."

"Okay. Thank you. We're done."

"We are?"

"Yes. I'll write up my report, but with multiple eyewitnesses, this case is closed. Death by suicide."

"Not according to those who knew him the best."

"Sometimes people have secrets. Do you have secrets, Max?"

"None I'm willing to share."

Dai cracked the faintest of smiles then was all business. "Don't interfere. Don't get people's hopes up that this is more than it appears. We'll look into Neil's background to try to discover why he did this, but there is no murder investigation. Am I clear?"

"As your blue eyes," I said, batting my own, now almost green from the sun.

"We'll be gone in half an hour, then this ridiculous event can continue. No need to keep the place sealed off."

"Wow! Great. Freya will be pleased, although I'm surprised Susie wanted it to go ahead."

"See, this is what I'm talking about. You're already wondering if it was her, aren't you?" Dai leaned forward. The table creaked, but he ignored it.

"No. I was just saying it's a shock, and I assumed she'd want to cancel."

"People do strange things. This is for her sister. Let her get through the grief however she can."

"Yes, of course. Um, thanks. I wasn't expecting this."

"Just because I'm a serious, unfriendly man, doesn't mean I'm utterly devoid of compassion."

"Of course not."

Dai ignored me and began writing. The interview was clearly over.

Anxious hopped up when I stood, but rather than following he sat beside DI Davies and barked a greeting. Dai smiled when he thought nobody was looking, and patted Anxious gently then reached into his pocket and handed him a biscuit. Anxious wagged happily as he took it, then trotted over to me.

My eyes locked with Dai's and he winked then put a finger to his lips.

I nodded in return, and together Anxious and I went to find everyone. Uncle Ernie wasn't far away, but he was alone.

"Where are the others?"

"Gone for a glass of wine to calm their nerves. I said I'd wait for you so I could give you your clothes. Max, the DI said it was suicide and this is closed."

"I know."

"So that's it?"

"According to him."

"Susie's beside herself. Doesn't know what to think."

"Neither do I," I admitted. "What should we do?"

"You're asking me?"

"You're older, wiser, and know them both better. What do Freya and Susie want to happen?"

"Freya wants the wedding, Susie, too, but we're convinced this was no suicide."

"Really?"

"Yes. Max, I know it makes no sense, but you didn't meet the guy. He was too full of his own self-importance to even consider it. Trust me, whatever happened, he wasn't suicidal."

"So either he was forced to do it, or somehow, despite what we think we saw, he was up there for another reason and was pushed?"

"That about sums it up." Uncle Ernie laughed and declared, "Nephew, you have your most puzzling case yet."

"Seems that way," I grumbled, wondering where on earth I should begin, or had I started already?

"Anxious, any ideas?" I asked.

The smartest Jack Russell this side of the border brushed the short grass with his tail, smiled, then barked.

"Good idea," I laughed. "Let's get ready for the big event, grab a bite to eat, and see what the day brings."

"That's the spirit! Let me go and get the outfits for you guys, then you can get changed, and hopefully I can marry the love of my life."

Uncle Ernie moved to leave, but I put a hand to his arm and asked, "You're sure about this? The wedding? It's the right move? Freya seems like a lovely woman, but it's a big commitment."

Uncle Ernie nodded repeatedly, then removed his hat and spread his arms wide. "Max, look at me. I'm a skinny ska nut who plays in a band that will never amount to more than it already has. I'm fine with that, and have made my peace because it's what I love and all I know. I'm over fifty, wrinkled, on the road half the time, have lost most of my hair, and thought I'd spend the rest of my life singing in the band until it got too ridiculous and my hips gave out, then while away the last few years at home reliving the past and listening to LPs like a dinosaur. Freya changed all that. I really love her. She loves me. We've talked a lot, and I mean a lot, and we both want the same thing out of life."

"And what's that?"

"To be happy, of course. What else is there?"

"Then you have my blessing," I teased.

Surprisingly, his eyes welled with tears and he took both my hands in his. They were shaking. "Max, I know you were joking around, but that means so much to me. Thank you."

"You deserve to be happy. Everyone does. Now, where are the clothes?"

"I'll go and get them."

Uncle Ernie hurried off so we waited a few minutes until he returned, then said we'd be back soon and made our way across the grass then over the river and stopped to admire the cathedral again before heading to the car park and Vee.

I really was too attached to the old campervan, as I got butterflies the closer we got. Was this normal, or should I see the campervan psychiatrist to have my head serviced and the oil changed?

With a chuckle, I opened Vee. Anxious jumped in and immediately settled on the bench seat despite the heat. I turned on the fan for us both and sat beside him, stroking his head as he slowly drifted off. I was tempted to do the same, but knew we only had a short while before the ceremony so had best get my skates on.

Something caught my eye, so I eased Anxious' head back onto the bench then stood in an awkward half crouch as the pop up top wasn't raised and shuffled forward.

"What's that?" I mumbled, peering over the driver's seat at something on the windscreen. The instant, deep, almost primordial dread of a parking ticket got my heart beating fast, but I had my ticket displayed so it couldn't be that. Nevertheless, I hurried outside and stood staring at the brown envelope jammed under the wiper of the split-screen.

Trying to catch the culprit was pointless, but I scanned the area anyway. Just tourists, people hurrying with dogs, and others driving around the full car park hoping for a lucky break.

I carefully eased the tape off the glass, pleased there was no sticky residue, then studied the envelope. Thick brown paper, A4, with string and a small tab to seal it rather than it being stuck down. I unwound the string, sniffed as I opened it, getting a familiar whiff of an aftershave I didn't know. This was the same person who had left the knife outside Vee last week and smashed the window with the mortar, but left the pestle next to Min as she slept with Anxious in her lap.

"I guess this isn't over," I muttered. Min had half-convinced me that once this mystery person had finished with their fun and games at the festival they'd leave me alone, but I hadn't told her about the knife they'd left, or the threatening note that accompanied it, and now I knew there was no way this was done. What was the end game though? Just intimidation, or something more physical?

I'd racked my brain trying to think who it might be, but had come up with nothing conclusive. I'd certainly had several intense encounters over the years as a chef in top restaurants, and sometimes it had got physical. Usually when I'd reluctantly sacked somebody, but there were also several cases of other chefs taking a swing at me because of disagreements over menus or choice of ingredients. The top-tier of fine-dining was a cutthroat business and it brought out the worst in some people, including me at times.

But that was in the past, and I'd been out of the game for well over a year now. There was nobody I could think of who would take things this far. I had a genuine stalker. They'd followed me to Chucklefest then drove right across Wales to leave me whatever was in the envelope. That was extreme, and very concerning. I sighed; there was nothing I could do about it but keep my guard up and be ready to defend myself if it came to that.

After another look around, I reluctantly peered into the envelope, expecting to see a note.

"Pebbles?" I frowned as I cupped my hand then carefully upended the contents. A selection of small stones varying in size from a grain of rice to a marble nestled in my palm, glinting in the sunlight. They were multi-coloured and very pretty, but what significance did they hold, if any?

I was clueless, and that rankled as much as anything. The master amateur detective couldn't solve the riddle of his own persecution. I carefully returned the stones to the envelope, wound up the string, then put it in the drawer next to the knife and notes already there. It was beginning to be quite a collection, and I wondered what was next. Hopefully nothing, but I knew better.

With a cool drink in hand, I leaned against the front of Vee and watched the world go by for five minutes to calm down and get my head in the right place. This was a day of celebration despite the terrible events of earlier, and I had to be in good spirits for Uncle Ernie and remember not to judge those getting their dogs married, however bizarre it seemed to me.

Once my nerves had settled, and I had to repeatedly fight the urge to call Min and tell her about the morning, I returned to find Anxious upside down, legs akimbo, head hanging over the side with his tongue lolling. I stifled a chuckle, as however many times I found him like that it always brought a smile to my face. I couldn't imagine my life without him, and it really hit home how different an experience my vanlife would be without the little cheeky chappy by my side.

Counting my blessings, and feeling better about things now I'd had a drink and was determined not to let my stalker ruin things, I pulled out the clothes from the bag Uncle Ernie had given me and smiled.

"Looks like he even got our sizes right," I told Anxious as he stirred and sat up to see what was happening. I held his outfit against him, then mine against me, and grinned.

Ten minutes later, we were outside Vee and I locked up. I took a photo of us and checked it over, pleased with the result. I was an Uncle Ernie clone with shiny shoes, white socks, black drainpipe trousers, white Fred Perry polo shirt with blood-red braces, and he'd even got me a trilby with a white band and a feather.

But, as usual, Anxious was the star of the show, and I knew he'd be fighting off suitors once they got a look at him. He sported a tiny, bespoke T-shirt that slid over his body easily with his two front legs through the holes. It was black, with white stripes mimicking braces, and he looked the part.

He paraded around in front of me, barking happily, tail wagging, and moved easily so it wasn't constricting as I'd worried.

"Min will love this photo. I'll send it now, even though we promised not to get in touch while she's away, then let's go have something to eat at the buffet by the ruin before the big day really gets started. Keep a lookout for anything strange, although, er, that might be difficult with so many people and animals. There are sure to be some outrageous outfits."

Anxious wagged in the affirmative, then hopped onto the grass and barked to tell me to hurry up in case all the sandwiches were gone before we arrived.

Min replied with a shocked smiley face, and it lifted my spirits more than it probably should have.

Chapter 5

Back at the ruins of the Bishop's Palace, it was apparent that DI Dai Davies had been true to his word — there was absolutely no sign of the police whatsoever. It made the whole scene even more surreal, as with Neil gone, no crime scene tape, no bored coppers, or people being asked questions, it was as though nothing had happened.

Guests were excited about the upcoming nuptials. Couples were crooning over smartly dressed dogs, single men more flamboyant than their perfectly coiffed pooches were parading around as though they were in the finals at Crufts. Everyone was enjoying themselves. Dressed in their finery, looking like they were the ones to be married, not the dogs, and I could only assume this was part of the whole experience. Tuxedos abounded, but so did outlandish costumes in garish colours, although hats were the main focus. The beautiful weather afforded the perfect opportunity to buy expensive and utterly impractical headwear and flaunt it.

I checked my watch. An hour to go. Time to eat.

Anxious was beyond bewildered by the number of dogs and people, and remained close, unsure what to do. Normally he'd go and play, but the choice was so overwhelming, and the dogs were beyond excited, not to mention confused, so he stuck with what he knew.

We made it to the buffet and I loaded a plate for myself and a smaller one for my always hungry companion, then we settled in the shade against a wall and munched on, or in the case of a certain someone, inhaled, our lunch.

"Mind if I join you?" asked a woman wearing identical clothes to me.

"Not at all. Please, take a seat."

"I'm guessing that what with the matching clobber, you must be Max."

"I am. Nice to meet you. You must be Rachel, Freya's best friend, and this must be Two-tone."

The brown Lab bounded around excitedly then lowered her front legs, bum in the air, and barked for Anxious to play. He looked to me for guidance and I gave the go-ahead, so he leapt up, licked his plate hurriedly just in case there happened to be an invisible sandwich, then they raced around the grass, staying close but enjoying themselves.

"They seem to be hitting it off straight away," said Rachel as she sat then sighed as the shade enveloped her. "Wow, that's much cooler. It's way too hot out here today. You picked the perfect spot."

"It's been a long day and I've had plenty of sun already. Have you just arrived?"

"About half an hour ago. I can't believe what happened. Neil's really dead? He jumped?"

"He's definitely dead. Nobody's too sure about the jumping part though."

"That's what Freya said, and Ernie. They're finishing getting ready, and her sister was there too. All three reckon something happened and he was murdered. But then they said you and Ernie saw him jump."

"It's confusing and a real mystery."

"Max, Ernie told me all about you. I checked out your wiki page and you're quite the sleuth."

"Don't believe everything you read. My dad wrote it, and he spends way too much time updating the entries."

"But you did solve those cases, right?"

"Yes, but not always by anything more than luck."

"And I bet the ladies swoon when you do the big reveal. A big strapping man like you with those muscles and that deep tan. I adore the look, by the way. Lovely wavy brown hair, bushy beard. You're my type." Rachel winked, and licked her lips, her feelings clear.

"Thanks for the compliment, and you're very pretty. I love the hairstyle and it's so blond."

"That's bottles for you," she laughed. "And don't feel uncomfortable. I'm a real flirt, but I know I'm about twenty years older than you."

"You don't look it."

"Liar!" she teased, flinging her head back, revealing a slender, line-free neck as smooth as her face. For a woman over fifty, she truly did seem very youthful with a slim figure, the hint of a tan on otherwise pale skin, dark eyes, and a snub nose with round cheeks making her almost cherubic despite her narrow frame.

"It's true. You aren't the same age as Freya and Uncle Ernie, are you?"

"I am. Me and Freya have been best friends since we were tiny kids. Grew up in the same street, were into the same music, same boys, same everything. We've been close ever since."

"That's so nice to have a best friend like that. Can I ask you a question?"

"Shoot," she grinned, then laughed as Anxious leaped over Two-tone and she responded by jumping, spinning three-sixty, then flopping onto her belly as Anxious vaulted her again.

"What do you think about the wedding?"

"All the dogs, you mean?" Rachel shrugged. "It's fun, you know? Freya and Susie have been running these events for years, and I'm so proud of them. We figured it was time for the two doggie best friends to get married. I know people think it's nutty, but there's no harm in it. Days like this are good for their business, although they don't earn as much as the single events, which is why they only do a few a year to help spread the word."

"Um, that's not what I meant, although it's great that the two of you are getting your dogs married, sure. I meant Freya and Uncle Ernie."

Rachel's eye twitched and she pursed her lips slightly before brightening. "It's what they want, and I'm happy for them both. I know it's sudden, but Freya's been chasing Ernie around the country like a lovesick teen for the last year. She's got a real thing for him, and they clicked instantly. He's a nice guy."

"He really is. A great uncle and a great man. But do you think it's too sudden? Are they going to regret this?"

Rachel shrugged. "Max, who knows? What have they got to lose? I had my doubts, and guess I still do, as they've been together just weeks, but I support Freya and hope they make a go of it."

"Then I guess we're on the same page with this. It just came as a shock. But they both seem happy, and that's the main thing. What about you? Are you married?"

"No. Never got hitched. I had a long-term partner for nigh on two decades, but five years ago it turned sour when he hit fifty and decided he didn't want this beautiful woman but preferred a dumb bimbo in her thirties who still hadn't learned how to tie her own shoelaces or read an analogue clock."

"You're joking, right?"

"I wish I was. His loss. It's actually been good for me. I'm an independent woman now. Freya and I spend a lot of time together, which is great."

"I assume you know my story?" I asked.

"Are you kidding? Ernie gave me the whole tale. About how you messed up but sold everything after your divorce and are now a full-time vanlifer. I'm envious and have thought about it myself, but I like my home comforts too much."

"You should give it a try. It might surprise you."

"Maybe I will. Once Freya and Ernie are married, I doubt I'll see her as much as I used to. We go to all the gigs together, and that's our thing."

"Ernie's always out on the road, so I'm sure you'll both get to travel with him and the band and see even more gigs," I reassured.

"Maybe." Rachel's eyes drifted and her bubbly personality seemed to evaporate. "I hope so."

"Are you okay?"

"Yes, fine." She turned and smiled, but admitted, "I just worry I'm about to lose my bestie. Is that silly?"

"Not at all. But I don't think Freya's the type to ditch a friend, even if it is for a skinny guy who goes by the name 'Elbows' because they're always so red and stick out all the time."

We laughed, and she punched me playfully on the arm like we were old friends. "When you say it like that, I'm certain she'll ditch me."

"Seriously, though, Ernie's a great man and I can tell you and Freya mean a lot to each other. You'll be fine."

"There you are!" gasped a very red, very frazzled looking Uncle Ernie as he shook his head and rubbed at his grey stubble.

"Hey, what's up?" I asked, frowning.

"What's up!? I'm getting married in less than an hour and we haven't sorted anything out. Freya's off organising the dog owners and finalising things with the agency staff, Susie's trying to keep it together but keeps crying even though she insists on staying to give Freya away along with Rachel, and I haven't even given you the ring or explained what you have to do."

"Then let's do that now. Don't worry, it will be fine."

"Ernie, you need to relax!" chuckled Rachel, jumping to her feet like a gymnast.

"Wow, how did you do that?" I asked, shocked. "You didn't even use your hands."

"I used to be into all kinds of sports when young, but now I just go to a weekly gymnastics group for the, er, more mature woman."

"Rachel used to be on the national gymnastics team. She was one of the best into her late twenties, then taught for a while. She's too modest to say how good she is."

"I'm not exactly a bashful woman, but I don't like to show off either. I can still do moves on the floor and am decent on the high bar, but my competing days are far behind me."

"That's something to be really proud of."

"Thanks." Rachel turned to Uncle Ernie. "Now, you smart fella, it's not your style to be getting so stressed. I'm sure everything is under control. All you have to do is stand there and look handsome."

"She's such a charmer," said Uncle Ernie, visibly relaxing as he winked.

"She is," I agreed. "So, what do you want me to do?"

"I want you to stop me having a meltdown. You look smart, Max. Less like a hippy, more like me."

"I love looking like a hippy, and I miss my Crocs already, but for you, anything. Have you seen Anxious?"

Uncle Ernie turned to watch the dogs go crazy and smiled happily. "He looks smarter than either of us. Thanks for this."

"My pleasure."

"That reminds me. I have to get Two-tone ready for the wedding. I'll see you guys soon. Ernie, don't worry. We have this under control. I know what I have to do, Freya and Susie made sure of that, so chill, okay?"

"I'll try."

With a wave, Rachel called Two-tone and they left. Anxious trotted over, eyes gleaming, and sat before Uncle Ernie, tail swishing as always, waiting to be adored.

"You're so handsome, Anxious." Uncle Ernie winked as he bent and wolf-whistled, which seemed to delight the ska-dog, who immediately paraded back and forth to more words of admiration.

"Okay, you two, let's get this wedding ready," I said.

"Am I doing the right thing, Max?"

"Of course. You said you were sure. If you are, so am I. You aren't having second thoughts, are you?"

"Last minute jitters, I suppose. And I can't get bloody Neil off my mind now. Why'd he have to go and spoil it?"

"To be fair to Neil, I don't think he did it to ruin your day. Especially if, like you insist, he didn't jump."

"What do you think of Rachel, eh? Bit of a handful, and a right flirt, isn't she? I bet she propositioned you."

"She did, but only in a lighthearted way. She knew about Min, and didn't pretend otherwise, so was only messing around."

"That's her style. She's a lovely lady. Her and Freya are really tight."

"Do you know she's worried about losing Freya once you get married? Has it caused any problems?"

"No problems. Freya put her mind at ease and promised they'd still hit the gigs and be as close as ever. I even had a word and told her she was always welcome at our shows and I wouldn't get between them."

"That was nice of you. So, what do we have to do first?"

"Um, not sure. Ah, the ring!" Uncle Ernie patted his pockets, panic rising as he failed to find it, then sighed as he pulled out the case from his front pocket. He lifted the lid to show me the simple gold band and grinned sheepishly. "What do you think?"

"Perfect. But it's not meant to impress, it's meant to be a symbol of your love, right? Just like mine." I showed him my wedding ring.

"You never took yours off, did you?"

"No chance."

"But Min did."

"That was different. She was so annoyed with me that she removed it before we were even divorced. That's when I'll know she's willing to come back to me. When she wears it again."

"She's already willing, Max. I can see it in her eyes when she looks at you. I've never known a couple hold hands as much as you pair. Certainly not a divorced couple."

"We're getting there." I took the ring, pocketed it, and asked, "What next?"

"We need to make sure everything is ready. Let's go check out the front entrance to the Bishop's Palace, as we're doing it right there in the doorway."

"Sounds cool. Very dramatic."

"Hey, when you pay what we did to be able to use this place for the afternoon, you'd want to get your money's worth. But actually," Uncle Ernie moved in close and checked nobody was eavesdropping, then whispered, "the amount everyone's forking out to get their dogs hitched means the wedding hasn't cost us a penny and we're in profit."

"Now that's how to do it," I laughed.

"Sure is. My Freya and Susie have done so well. Rachel was miffed she wasn't part of the business at first, but she got over it."

"How come she wasn't?"

"Because they wanted to do it together, and sometimes three's a crowd, I guess. But mostly I think it was because Rachel isn't the best with money and doesn't have a business head on her shoulders. I think there was a slight falling out, but nothing too heavy. They're still the best of friends and it's all water under the bridge."

"Sometimes friendship and business don't mix. But sometimes the same can be said for family. It's a risk to work with either."

"I wouldn't do it. Too much to argue over. But Freya and Susie are on the same wavelength. It was only ever Neil that caused bother for them. Always trying to get Susie to quit, never supporting her, and he refused to help them start up with any of his money. He was one of those guys who gave Susie housekeeping money but kept most for himself."

"Very old school and still how plenty of people are. It's not how I would do things, but lots of couples have separate bank accounts."

"That's fine, and sometimes sensible, but treating someone like your personal hired help is pushing things too far."

"Far enough to want them dead?" I wondered.

"Don't say something like that in front of Freya or Susie. They'll go ape. This is our special day, Max, so don't wind them up."

"I wouldn't dream of it. But you have to admit, it makes Susie the prime suspect. And Rachel's a gymnast so could have climbed the wall easily and got down in record time. She might still be angry about being left out of the business and this is her revenge."

"I can't see any of them doing it. And why not let it be a suicide rather than press the issue, insisting he was killed? That doesn't make sense."

"True," I admitted. "Come on, let's ensure everything is going to run smoothly then get you hitched. Are you nervous?"

"More nervous than I've been in years. I can stand on stage in front of hundreds of people and get a little jittery, but this is different. I'm this close to freaking out!" Uncle Ernie pinched his fingers together, grinned at me, then shook his head. "Max, I'm a mess," he admitted with a short, staccato bark. "A man of my age and I'm about to lose it."

"I'm here, and nothing bad will happen. I know you're going to do well, and Freya's a lucky woman. Everything looks amazing."

We paused beside the registration table which had now been cleared of name tags and stacks of documents, replaced with certificates waiting to be handed out to the proud "parents" of the dogs. A marriage certificate with their names handwritten, the stack thick. Some were in frames I assumed people paid extra for, but most were just the document that people could do with as they wished.

Outside the Bishop's Palace, things were looking incredible. Susie had recovered enough to finalise last-minute details and was re-arranging a huge garland of flowers hung above the entrance. Strewn across the steps were rose petals leading down to the white chairs facing what was to all intents and purposes a miniature stage with the dark, brooding doorway the perfect frame for the newlyweds.

Flowers adorned each chair, bright ribbons and streamers hung from every available wall and ran high above the seats, making it a truly festive affair.

"Doesn't it look awesome?" I gasped, amazed how quickly it had been transformed.

"They know their business," beamed Uncle Ernie, his shoulders relaxing. "I can't wait to marry this gal."

"You deserve to be happy. Feel better now?"

"Much. I could do with a drink to calm my nerves though."

"Sure thing. Let's go and get one. And what happens after the weddings?"

"We have a big buffet here, then we're having a party on the beach. The ladies have sorted it out. The guys from the band are coming this evening, so we'll play a few tunes and have a right royal knees up."

"But they aren't coming to the actual wedding?"

"They had stuff on this afternoon. So did lots of people. It's fair enough, as I didn't exactly give anyone much notice."

"But at least they can make it for the evening party. Come on, let's get you that drink."

We wandered over to the temporary bar where drinks were already being laid out for anyone who wanted one. It seemed Uncle Ernie wasn't the only one feeling nervous, as the sea of faces of those waiting to get their dogs married looked more stressed than the only human about to tie the knot.

It was one of the most surreal drinks I'd ever had.

Chapter 6

Uncle Ernie nodded to the various men and women but was clearly dazed. They smiled and wished him well, but the bar was filled with nervous tension, and everyone had their own upcoming marriage on their mind. Part of me wanted to tease them and laugh at how they were behaving, but the other half of me understood that for those in attendance this was an important day and possibly the prime event of the year.

Uncle Ernie practically inhaled a glass of something fizzy while I sipped at mine, the chilled Prosecco welcome in the searing heat.

"Ah, that's better," he gasped, wiping his mouth and grinning. "I don't know what's wrong with me, but I want this to be over with. I'm finally doing it, Max. Getting married and settling down again."

"I don't think you'll ever settle down. Especially with Freya being as nuts about ska as you. You'll be on the road until they cart you off in a coffin."

"True," he chortled, then snatched another glass off the counter.

"Go easy on that. You don't want to be falling about when you say your vows."

"Maybe you're right." Uncle Ernie sipped rather than gulped, then leaned against the counter.

I joined him, and together we watched the last of the decorations go up. The place was buzzing with tourists as well as pets and owners, a party vibe as we got closer to the actual weddings.

Susie was barking orders at local temp agency staff, flustered but clearly in her element as she ticked things off on a clipboard whilst casting an eye over every aspect of the scene for imperfections. The seats began to fill up as assistants ushered everyone into place, the first rows reserved for family and friends, then the rest for the nervous owners and their dogs. Ernie explained that they were arranged in order of when they would get their moment in the limelight.

An argument broke out beside us between two men, then one stormed off with a very pampered poodle, the remaining man cradling a chihuahua like it might be stolen. He glanced our way and hurried over, stroking the dog and soothing it as you would a baby.

"Did you see that?" he gasped, shaking his head and frowning as he glared at the back of the retreating man.

"Sorry, no. Is there a problem?" I asked, not keen to get involved but knowing this would be over sooner if I was polite.

"Marcus, not again. Can you please let this slide?" groaned Uncle Ernie.

"I did! It's him. He's trying to upstage me and my Buttercup."

"Buttercup?" I asked, not following.

"This adorable little creature here," beamed Marcus as he looked at the dog curled in his arms. "We're supposed to be getting married, but how can we when that impossible man is so insufferable?"

"Just relax," said Uncle Ernie. "Max, this is Marcus, and he's been having an issue with the owner of the dog Buttercup here is meant to be marrying. There's nothing wrong as far as I can tell, but Marcus believes he's being taken advantage of."

"Not believe. I know. The whole thing's ridiculous. That Susie doesn't know how to organise properly, and although I would never say a bad word about your Freya, even you have to admit that they're clueless."

"Marcus, watch your tone," warned Uncle Ernie, bristling. "They are doing a wonderful job and everyone's happy apart from you. If you have an issue with where you stand, you need to sort it with Patrick." He turned to me and explained, "Patrick is the owner of the other dog. It's the Poodle with the pink dye job. Marcus wants to stand on the left, but Patrick says that's the side he was promised."

"This is becoming an utter disaster. My Buttercup is so disappointed."

We watched the sleepy Chihuahua yawn, clearly bored by the whole affair, before he curled up tighter in Marcus' arms and groaned as his eyes closed.

"Why do you need to be on the left?" I was intrigued, despite being more concerned about Uncle Ernie than this man.

"Because it's his side. Buttercup always stands on the left. It's our thing. It's how he's been trained, so when they get married he'll understand what to do if he's on the correct side. But oh no, Freya and Susie insist it won't matter and that because of the way everything is laid out, all the males are on the right."

"To be fair, it is where you're meant to stand," I said. "Men are always on the right. Um, Buttercup's a male, yes?"

"Of course! Oh, it's no use. I suppose we'll have to manage. But know this, Ernie. I am most disappointed in you and your whole team."

"Hey, it's not my team. I'm nothing to do with it. You can't expect them to make changes like that. It's not how these things work. Patrick's correct that you're on the right. Everyone else has to do it, so why not you and Buttercup?"

"Because of his training!" wailed Marcus, flinging an arm into the air and nearly dropping the startled pooch.

Anxious barked a warning, but Marcus was oblivious to anything but his own concerns and slunk off in a huff with a curt, "Excuse me, coming through," to the dense crowds waiting to be seated by a flustered-looking Susie and the team.

"That man's an absolute nightmare. He's been on at me all day about this stupid left side thing. I told him it's nothing to do with me, but he insists on complaining."

"He's certainly a handful. Why would you only train your dog to do things on one side? And what are those things?" I wondered.

"Who knows? Most likely, he's been practising a trick to show off and now is put out because it won't work. But Freya said he's just one of those men who won't stop picking fault with things. Never happy. She's known him a few years. He's always on the circuit and too opinionated. He loves disagreeing with how they do things and never has a kind word to say about anyone."

"The circuit?" I asked, confused.

"Max, some people here have been going to animal weddings for years. They know each other, are friends, or in online forums, and they have their own chat groups. They spend way too much time sharing pictures, talking about the next group wedding, and angling for an invite to the most important events. It's a cutthroat business."

"I never knew. Amazing what goes on that you've never even heard about."

"Tell me about it. They love their animals, no doubt, but as much as anything it's a social thing. A chance to get together. There's endless backstabbing and rivalry. People want to be invited to the main events, especially the celebrity ones. And yes, I mean dog celebrities. Some of them have their own online channels with massive followings, and they're like one big, utterly deranged family. Desperate for likes on photos, angling for invites, making calendars and selling merchandise. It's big business for a few of them. But we don't even get the massive celebrities usually, just those who want a fun day out. But you get a few like Marcus who will never be satisfied."

"Has he always caused trouble for Freya and Susie?"

"Always. He's a real headache. He works for the same firm as Neil. You wouldn't think it to look at him, but Marcus is an utter beast when it comes to business. They were a powerhouse of a team. As ruthless as each other. Closed down more small businesses than anyone else in the company. But his real passion is his dog. He knows everyone and gets people to back him up, so the girls have had no end of issues. He's not a fan of Susie's, and I doubt he's even offered his condolences for Neil's death. He's so lost in his own stress-fest that he doesn't have any room for giving a hoot about anyone or anything else."

"Did he like Neil?"

"No way. Apparently, they were always arguing, and Neil hated that Marcus was so into the animals. It was a real bone of contention between them. The last few years, they hardly worked together at all. Only when their boss insisted."

"Think he's capable of shoving someone off a wall?"

"Marcus? No chance, mate. You're barking up the wrong tree there."

"It was worth asking. Just trying to get the broader picture."

"Sure, I understand, but not Marcus. He'd talk you to death, not shove you. In case you didn't notice," Uncle Ernie snorted, "he's not exactly the sporty type. I doubt he'd even get up onto the parapet."

"I guess you're right. Wow, these pet weddings are full of drama, aren't they?"

"You wouldn't believe me if I told you half the stories Freya recounts," laughed Uncle Ernie, pulling at his collar. "I'm so hot. I wish we could get this over with."

A smile spread across my face as music played quietly from the speakers, the volume increasing once the DJ knew everything was working properly. Mellow ska danced across the parched grass, filled the heavy air, and echoed off the ancient walls radiating heat onto the sweating, fidgeting gathering of over a hundred people.

"Looks like your wish has been granted," I said with a nod. "You ready?"

"Ready as I'll ever be. Max, don't let me do anything dumb." His eyes darted to the people sitting in the rows of chairs, those standing to the side, and the group still at the bar or helping themselves to the pre-wedding buffet that was now being cleared away hurriedly by harried staff.

"Like what?"

"Oh, I dunno. Start running, maybe? My feet seem to think they'd rather be in another country, and I'm so close to a panic attack I'm not sure I can feel my arms. Are they still attached?" Uncle Ernie frowned as his eyes lowered, but then he swayed and I feared he would collapse.

"They're still attached. All present and accounted for. What's got into you? You're always so cool under pressure."

"It's because I love Freya so much. Max, this is important, and I do not want to blow it."

"Come on, we have to go to the front. You look amazing, you even smell nice, and Freya's a lucky woman. Don't forget that."

"Thanks." Panic tore at my uncle as he rubbed his shoes against his trousers to shine them up, then he licked his palms, removed his hat and patted his buzzcut before dropping his trilby as he tried to fiddle with his braces.

I retrieved it, put it on his head, and held him steady by the shoulders. "Relax. Enjoy it. Soon, you'll be a married man. You deserve this. You're doing great."

"What would I do without you? Okay, let's go."

I slid my arm through his to ensure he remained steady, but also so he didn't bolt, then I asked Anxious to lead the way. He did an abrupt about-turn, barked at the stragglers to clear the way, then we walked slowly to the rear of the rows of seats and down the aisle. Uncle Ernie kept his focus on the ground ahead, but I smiled and nodded at the sea of happy, hot, excited faces keen to get the party started.

Once at the front, we greeted the priest. A young woman with a generous smile and a shocking frizz of dry hair like a miniature bale of hay perched on her head. She smiled warmly from the top of the stairs, the white dog collar stark against her black clothes and the gloom of the interior.

We faced the aisle as the music grew louder. Susie beamed at us from the rear, then hurried off, presumably to get Freya. I noted Rachel, Freya's best friend, scowl as she watched Susie, then she attended to Two-tone who was as excited as the other animals by this strange human ritual.

Although the crowd was mostly quiet, half the animals were very rowdy. Barking, growling, sniffing, or trying to jump up at their owners. I wondered if seats were the right choice. Surely it would have been better if everyone was standing to give them more room? But I was certainly no wedding planner and assumed the professionals knew what they were doing.

Anxious took it all in his stride and remained sitting, watching with interest, resplendent in his tiny faux suit T-shirt.

The mellow ska track morphed into *Outer Space* by the Prodigy as Susie and Freya emerged from the screened-off gazebo. A white veil hid her face, her pigtails poked out either side, curled somehow like they had wires through them, which I suspected they did. The sisters' matching outfits were spotless, and when dealing with a hundred or more dogs it was an impressive feat.

Anxious stood and barked happily as Rachel joined them, and the three women walked elegantly down the aisle towards us. I could feel Uncle Ernie shaking through my arm still linked with his.

"You got this," I whispered with a smile and a wink.

"I do," he said, voice steady. "I can't believe this is happening."

"Your deserve it."

We took a step apart as they approached, and Uncle Ernie gasped as Freya stopped in front of him. She lifted her veil and smiled beautifully before lowering it again. I moved to one side with Susie and Rachel while the couple mounted the steps and stood with their backs to us while the vicar had a quiet word, then we were beckoned forth and took a single step up.

"Please be seated," asked the vicar, her voice mellow but carrying well.

Anxious was one of the first to sit, his position on the step the perfect spot to keep an eye on things. It took a while for the other animals to settle, but once it was as quiet as it was ever going to be, the music faded and the ceremony began.

When it was time for rings to be exchanged, I made a joke of panic-patting my pockets, causing Uncle Ernie to blanch, then handed him the ring with a chuckle. He laughed, a sharp bark of relief, then the vicar continued until both rings were worn and it was announced that they could kiss.

Freya lifted the veil and tucked it behind dancing pigtails, her face glowing. Susie smiled at her sister, wiped her eyes, and looked genuinely pleased. Rachel nodded and smiled, but there was no sparkle in her eyes.

"Yes!" Uncle Ernie twirled Freya, kissed her, and beamed, the happiest man alive.

One of the assistants threw dog-friendly confetti, apparently made of rice paper that would be used throughout the afternoon, as Anxious led the way back along the aisle, snaffling it as he went. We followed behind, chatting excitedly and everyone grinning from ear to ear.

Things got rather out of hand once the dogs realised there were treats covering the grass, albeit utterly bland ones, so it was a free-for-all for a while and we had to dodge slapping tails, a lot of legs, and even more drool.

"Maybe that wasn't the best idea," laughed Freya, but she clearly didn't care.

I caught sight of Marcus near the back with his beloved dog in his arms, eyes locked on Susie and flashing angrily at the perceived injustice of his upcoming marriage. Rachel was smiling and talking to Susie about how well it went, but I noted her clenched hands and the way she kept glancing into the crowds as though expecting something to happen.

As we reached the end of the aisle, Uncle Ernie and Freya turned and called, "Thank you for coming!"

People clapped and cheered, wolf-whistled, and congratulated them.

Freya released Uncle Ernie's hand for a moment and waved for calm. Once things had settled, she said, "Thank you so much for making this a special day. We'll have a short half hour interlude to prepare everything for the rest of the weddings, then each of your registered pets will be married in the order you have already been given. After that, there's a buffet and then this evening a party on the beach where everyone is invited. There will be wedding cakes, both for humans and animals, and the dogs can run free and have a wonderful time. See you soon."

The cheers and applause were even louder this time as everyone jumped up from their seats and headed to the free bar to get a drink before the event continued.

Uncle Ernie pulled me to one side once we entered the private gazebo where drinks and a selection of snacks for our intimate party had been laid out. It was very professional, with nice floral touches, and I could see why their services were in high demand. Especially considering they did pet weddings, not people ones.

"You did awesome," I said, meaning it. "I'm so proud of you. How do you feel?"

"Like a very lucky guy. Thanks so much for helping me out. I think I'd have collapsed if you weren't there to keep me upright."

"You'd have been fine." Freya joined us and we kissed, then I congratulated her and also told Susie how well she'd done organising everything and holding it together like she had. She was flagging, but managed to smile and was clearly pleased for her sister.

Rachel beamed at her friend, agreeing how well she and Susie had done and that it had been a beautiful moment.

"There was only one thing missing," lamented Uncle Ernie, shaking his head.

"I know, and I don't understand what's got into them. I tried calling a few times, but either they have no signal, are out of charge, or something's gone wrong."

"They should be here. He promised."

A horn beeped, and I sighed as I turned to Uncle Ernie and with raised eyebrows said, "Guess who?"

Chapter 7

A crowd had gathered on the grass near to the Bishop's Palace so we hurried over, both of us knowing who would make such an entrance at the most inappropriate time in this utterly outlandish way.

Anxious took the lead, excited and yipping, clearing a path as wedding guests returned to the business of glaring at each other and vying for the best seat for when it was their turn.

We stumbled forward into empty ground and stared, open-mouthed, at the scene before us.

Dad was sitting behind the handlebars of an ancient sixties motorbike gifted by a woman we'd met in the most peculiar of circumstances. I'd been shocked when he'd followed through with the offer of the motorbike and sidecar, believing he'd never get around to it. But I was wrong, and it seemed like he and Mum had finally decided to use it.

Dad removed his helmet and goggles and beamed at us. I waved back, smiling and shaking my head at the sight of my maverick father. As usual, he was dressed in his fifties attire. A white cotton T-shirt with the sleeves rolled up, indigo Levi's 501s with fat turn-ups, and his hair slicked back with just about all the Brylcreem into a tight quiff. He ran his steel comb through his shiny locks as he turned to his partner in crime, my mum, who somehow, and I couldn't quite believe it, had managed to squeeze into the sidecar of this antique vehicle.

Dad said something to Mum and she nodded then unfastened the strap of her helmet, removed it, yanked the goggles off, then shook out bright red dyed hair. She hurriedly tied a black and white bandana around her head and gave Dad a glare that would go down in history as utterly epic.

People actually oohed and aahed, and Uncle Ernie and I gasped as we watched the air incinerate as her death stare traversed the short distance between the pair. Dad tried to duck, but it was too little, too late, and he was hit with the full force of Mum's ire. He toppled sideways, grabbed for the handlebars but missed, and ended up in a heap, legs akimbo, on the grass.

Anxious took it as his cue to launch and have a play, so barked excitedly then raced forward and leaped onto my startled father as he rubbed at his head. My best buddy hurriedly recounted the day's events, then decided a quick lick would be more fun, so attacked Dad with gusto.

"A little help here," shouted Mum as she pushed and heaved at the sidecar but was seemingly stuck fast.

We rushed to assist, and after a quick hello which was met with nothing but an icy glare for Dad and a warm smile for us, we grabbed hold of Mum's bare arms carefully and managed to extricate her from the tiny sidecar.

Mum pinged out like a cork from a bottle of shaken Prosecco and we sprawled onto the grass. Knowing this was not how she liked to make her entrance, we got her upright in record time and then she literally popped to full size.

Any sensible soul would have worn jeans or possibly even leather safety trousers in a dangerous sidecar, but my mother was neither sensible nor any other person and had standards that were adhered to at all times. Her trademark polka dot dress fluffed out like it knew the trouble it would be in otherwise, and the wide-hemmed white dress with reds dots to match her hair—with matching shiny red high heels, of course—flared. For good measure, Mum shook like a wet dog then twirled to ensure her outfit resumed its rather flamboyant and certainly eye-catching true size and shape.

"How did you manage to fit in there?" asked Uncle Ernie, eyes bugging.

"I had to squeeze her in," said Dad, brushing himself down and joining us. "It was like shoving a cake into an egg cup."

"Don't you compare me to a cake!" warned Mum, eyes beginning to smoulder.

Dad ducked and said, "You look ace, love. Gorgeous as ever."

"And don't try to sweet talk me after what you just put me through. I am never going in that death trap again. I don't know what possessed me to let you talk me into the stupid thing."

"It's a classic. They don't make them like this any more."

"No, and now we know why. Ridiculous!" Rant over, Mum smiled at us and we hugged.

Dad slapped me and Uncle Ernie on the back, grinned, and said, "Sorry we're late. I hope we didn't miss anything."

"You missed the wedding," I said.

"It just finished," said Uncle Ernie.

"What!? Damn, I'm so sorry. We left early, too, and I figured we had plenty of time. The motorbike isn't as fast as I thought, though, and someone," Dad glanced at Mum, "insisted we take what she called the scenic route. Meaning, we got lost."

"We did not get lost. I didn't want to die on the main roads, so we came the slower but less deadly way." Mum beamed at Uncle Ernie and asked, "Was it a lovely wedding? Did she say yes?"

"Of course she said yes! I wished you could have both been here, but Max did a wonderful job as my best man and he didn't even lose the ring."

"You should have been here," I told my folks, "but at least you're here now. There's still the rest of the weddings, then the buffet, then the party later on."

"We're so sorry, Ernie," said Dad. "I really wanted to be here to see my brother get hitched. Where's the unlucky lady?" he asked, laughing as he punched his arm.

"Here I am," declared Freya, frowning as she eyed up Mum's impressive dress, clearly miffed that she might be upstaged.

"Freya! How wonderful." Mum hurried over on rather shaky legs, then hugged Freya before standing back, looking her up and down, and declaring, "You look wonderful. I love the matching outfits. You must be so happy."

"Thanks, Jill. It's sweet of you to say so. You look lovely too. Such a beautiful, and very big, dress." Freya glanced at the sidecar then back to Mum, clearly as shocked she'd fitted in as everyone else.

"You're such a dear. And now we're sisters-in-law. Is that right? Are we if you're Jack's sister-in law?"

"I think so," said Freya. "But let's say we're sisters. That sounds so much better."

"Really? That's great."

"So, who died?" The mood darkened as Dad's words hit home. Slowly, his smile faded and he looked at us in turn before asking, "Someone did? Max, I was only fooling around as you're always getting into bother lately, but someone died?"

"Was it a murder?" asked Mum brightly, oblivious to the change in mood.

"Of course it was a murder," sighed Dad. "Max keeps getting involved in them and so do we whenever we meet up. I can't believe I helped solve two murders now," he beamed. "If I help with this one, that'll make three."

"You did not help solve the last one," scolded Mum. "My Max solved it and you know that. And look what came of that awful death. The stupid motorbike and sidecar."

"I did help solve it. Tell her, Max."

"Dad, you helped figure out the first one, but I'm not sure you contributed the other week. Maybe a little," I conceded, "but remember, you were ill with food poisoning. Anyway, it doesn't matter. It's great to see you both."

"Great to see you too, Son. Now, what happened?"

At that moment, Susie arrived, looking surprisingly upbeat and with a genuine warm greeting for everyone. "Jack! Jill! You made it. So nice to see you again."

"Hello, Susie," said Mum before enveloping her in a hug, her preferred way of greeting friends and strangers alike.

"Don't leave me cuddleless," warned Dad with a cheesy grin, then he scooped Susie up and hugged her tight. "We were just telling the others that we're sorry we're late, but at least we have the rest of the day to enjoy. It's such a shame to miss my brother's wedding though."

"Yes, it is a shame, and it was wonderful. Freya's so pretty, and Ernie's such a wonderful man. But you're here now, and that's the main thing. Gosh, did you really come in that?"

All eyes turned to the old motorbike and sidecar. Anxious and Special went over for a sniff, then Anxious barked, most likely telling him it was safe as he'd ridden in it before in a very dramatic way. As if to prove his point, he jumped into the sidecar and Special backed away, barked, but then decided to risk it and joined my grinning pooch.

"Anxious, don't get it dirty. Mum has to go home in it," I warned.

"I am not going home in that foul thing! I'll stay here until somebody takes pity on me and gives me a lift."

"I can take you home if you want," I offered.

"Aw, that's so sweet, but then your dad will be lonely and he'll most likely go on and on about it for weeks and weeks. No, thank you, love, but I suppose I better suffer and go with your father."

"You won't suffer as much as I will," mumbled Dad.

"I heard that!"

"No, you didn't," countered Dad, stepping away and using me as a shield against Mum's demonic eyes. He turned back to Susie and asked, "Everything okay, love? You look great, same as everyone does, but is there something up?" When nobody spoke, Dad clearly worked out the issue and asked kindly, "Do you want to talk about it? I know we've only met the once, but we're here for you."

"Course we are," said Mum, not wanting to be left out. "You're family now. Freya's sister is basically my sister, so we're all one big, happy family."

"Not so happy at the moment," mumbled Susie. "But I don't want to put a downer on the day."

"Susie, your husband is dead," said Freya, putting her arm around her.

"Dead?" asked Dad. "As in... er, kicked the bucket dead?"

"What other kind of dead is there, you stupid man?" sighed Mum. "What happened, love?"

"He was pushed from up there!" sobbed Susie, pointing to the impressive wall, her composure breaking down completely.

"The police insist it was a suicide as nobody saw anyone else up there with him," I explained.

"But it wasn't, was it?" asked Dad, trying to hide his excitement at the chance to be involved in yet another murder mystery.

"We don't think so," said Uncle Ernie. "Neil wasn't the kind of bloke to top himself, and we're convinced something's going on. We just don't know what."

"But Max will solve this, won't you?" asked Susie, eyes pleading as she hugged her sister.

"I'll do my best, but I can't promise anything. It's a very strange case, and I'm not sure where to begin."

"Of course he'll figure it out," said Mum, like it was a foregone conclusion. "Our Max always finds the killer. Susie, this is awful, and on such an important day too. Whatever could have happened?"

"Mum, nobody knows. Susie's been very brave, and the police and a detective have already left. So many people saw him fall, but nobody noticed anything suspicious."

"Then we better go and take a look, hadn't we?" insisted Mum, getting that no-nonsense look that meant it would be pointless to argue.

"Max and I already went up onto the parapet," explained Uncle Ernie. "We had a good look around and all we found was litter and one strange item."

"What was that?" asked Mum and Dad, literally rubbing their hands together as they got caught up in the mystery instantly.

"A ring. A nice one, with a large diamond," I said. I showed them the photo on my phone and realised there was now no way they would back down from hunting for clues themselves.

"That's a pricey diamond," said Dad, as if he knew what he was talking about.

"How would you know?" asked Mum. "You never bought me a ring like that."

"It's a big diamond, so of course it's worth lots," grumbled Dad.

"I'll take them up there," I offered, knowing this wasn't how Uncle Ernie and Freya wanted to spend the first few minutes of their married life. "Uncle Ernie, why don't you and Freya go for a walk while Susie has a rest? Don't forget, there's a lot going on today, so you need time together too."

Uncle Ernie winked at me, then asked Freya, "Fancy a stroll, Mrs. Effort?"

"I'd be delighted," she grinned, taking his hand.

"I'll lie down for a while," mumbled Susie, then walked off in a daze without saying goodbye.

We watched her leave, but so did plenty of others. The guests were already rather antsy now the human marriage was over, keen to get their pets wed and enjoy the party afterwards, but everyone understood that after such a terrible event, the festivities would have to wait a while.

"You went ahead even after Neil died?" Dad asked Freya.

"We said we'd call it off, but Susie insisted we continue."

"Probably because she hated her husband," said Dad.

"It's true. He wasn't a nice man," said Freya, "but he was still her husband and it was a terrible shock. I can't say I'm sorry he's out of my sister's life, but I wouldn't wish him dead and neither would Susie."

"Of course she wouldn't," said Mum, tutting at Dad for being insensitive. "But from what we've heard about him, which is only what you've told us, mind you, she's better off without him. You can run the business without him acting like he's better than you, she can do what she wants with her own money, and she won't be belittled. That's what he was like, isn't it?"

"Yes, I'm afraid it was. But that doesn't mean we shouldn't solve this. We need to, for Susie. So she knows the truth."

"Maybe he did just jump," said Dad with a shrug.

"Not Neil. Never!" snapped Freya.

"Then let's get to it." Dad winked at me, keen to begin, so we left Freya and Uncle Ernie to have some peace then headed over to the building.

"Max, what's the deal here?" asked Dad, pulling me to a stop once we were alone.

"How'd you mean?"

"You know what he means," said Mum with a shake of her head.

"I honestly don't."

"It's obvious, isn't it?" Dad asked Mum.

"I thought so."

"Can you please just tell me? I honestly have no idea what you're both talking about."

"Susie or Freya offed that horrid man, Neil," said Mum, folding her arms across her chest and radiating smugness.

"Exactly," agreed Dad. "Where were they when he supposedly jumped? From what I've heard of the man, no way he would do that. He was too up himself, so someone had to push him."

"Dad, I saw the whole thing, and there was nobody there. If they were, they were an expert at hiding. He was right up on the wall with nobody around him. I can't explain it, but you're right about one thing. It does feel like it was murder."

"So it was Freya or Susie," said Dad.

"Why would Freya kill her sister's husband?"

"So he doesn't interfere with her business? To get her sister free of a bad husband."

"And Susie might have done it because she was fed up with his cheating, controlling ways. He was always belittling her, according to Freya. She's sweet, isn't she? We don't know her that well, and only met last week, but the wedding was a total surprise. Was it lovely?"

I smiled at my mother's ability to morph seamlessly from murder to weddings, so with a chuckle said, "Yes, it was lovely. They both looked great, and it went smoothly apart from the possible murder. But I can't picture Susie doing it, or Freya, and after he fell, they were right there within seconds."

"But was there enough time for them to scramble down from the wall and pretend they'd been somewhere else?" asked Dad.

"Possibly," I conceded. "They both said they were sorting things out for the wedding. There was a lot to do, but they had everything really well organised. Nobody else said they saw them as such, but then, nobody saw anyone come from inside the palace grounds as there were people everywhere."

"Then we better go take a look at where he fell from and see what we can find," insisted Dad.

"And I'm going to help solve this case," said Mum.

"I hope you do," I said, meaning it. I kissed Mum on the cheek. "Let's go and take another look, but be careful. Those shoes aren't the best for climbing, and we don't want any more accidents today."

"Son, I've been wearing high heels since before you were born. I can go anywhere and do anything in them."

"It's true," said Dad. "We once spent four days in the Lake District and she wore them everywhere, even up Skiddaw mountain."

"Then let's go." I led the way, wondering how on earth this could be anything but a suicide, but with that strange conviction that the truth would present itself at some point and this would make sense.

Chapter 8

"Here you go, love, let me give you a hand." Dad reached out to help Mum up the last section, but she ignored him and sprang onto the parapet with ease and landed with a click of her heels.

"I told you, I'm fine. Why are you so red and sweaty?"

"I'm not. Er, but it is hot up here. Bloomin' stone is baking. It's like an oven surrounded by these walls." Dad rubbed at his face and was clearly wondering the same thing as me. How come we were burning up and tired from the climb, but Mum remained fresh with her makeup and hair flawless. Never mind she was in high heels and an utterly impractical dress.

"Mum, you're fitter than ever. Have you been exercising more?" The moment I said it, I knew I was in for trouble as she whipped around and planted her legs wide, squared her shoulders, and gave me the look every son dreads. Dad shuffled behind me then turned his back for good measure. "Traitor," I hissed.

"No, Son, just sensible."

"Why would you say I needed more exercise? Are you saying I'm fat?"

"Of course not! I meant you got up here no problem, and aren't even sweating."

"Ah, so you're saying I was fat and unfit?"

"I'm not saying that either." I was going to lose this battle, but brightened as I added, "Dad looks knackered, doesn't he?"

Mum sniggered, her ire gone, and said, "Daft old pilchard needs to up his game."

"I am not a pilchard, and stop stealing my saying. That's what I call people. You know that."

"Pilchard," countered Mum expertly. "Now, Max, where did you find the ring? Think it's still there?"

"The police have it. The detective couldn't get up here, but an officer took photos then retrieved the evidence."

"What did you say was here apart from the ring?" asked Dad.

"Just an empty water bottle and a packet of crisps. Oh, and a kid's glove."

"Yes, but what kind? What brand of crisps and water bottle?"

"Wow, you want all the details? Let's have a look on my phone, but I think it was Walker's cheese and onion crisps and I'm not sure about the water."

We looked at the pictures and I realised it was a supermarket own brand water bottle, but that meant nothing as they were becoming more and more common now. But something was beginning to niggle at me and although I didn't know what it was, I got that tingle telling me to be ultra aware and remain open to any possibility.

"That's what you get with a meal deal at Sainsbury's," said Mum. "Did you find a sandwich container or maybe a pasta pot? What else do they offer?"

"Wraps, or even baguettes. And rolls. The little tubs with the pasta, too, don't they?" said Dad.

"I already said pasta."

"We didn't find anything else," I said.

"Then let's search again," insisted Dad.

"That's a great idea. Maybe they left the rest of their rubbish up here too. I don't know if it's relevant, but it might be."

"Son, I think it is," said Dad. "These places get cleaned regularly by the staff to make it nice for everyone. If there's rubbish up here, it's most likely from today, right?"

"Yes, but loads of people have been up here already. Tourists, plus all the guests."

"And Neil and whoever killed him," Mum reminded me.

"So are we saying the killer nipped off to Sainsbury's, got a meal deal, then ate it and left their rubbish then shoved manky Neil off the wall?" asked Dad.

"You can't call him manky Neil," I said. "And I doubt anyone would be so lax. Although, there is the ring, and that's a big deal."

"But it might not have been anything to do with Neil," said Mum. "Maybe someone proposed but got jilted and they lost the ring. Could have been up here for ages."

"That's what Uncle Ernie and I assumed. We need to keep an open mind about it all. But anyway, I'm glad you're both here. Shame you missed the big event though."

"We're really sorry about that. I wanted to see my younger brother get hitched more than anything. I feel awful about it. Think he'll forgive me?"

"Dad, of course he will. He wanted us together for his big day, but he knows what you're like."

"What am I like?" Dad bristled, but then he smiled and admitted, "We are often a little late, aren't we? Never seem to find places as easily as everyone else. But let's face it, it's what makes us so lovable."

"We are adorable, aren't we?" giggled Mum, giving Dad's arm a squeeze then pecking him on the cheek.

"You're both great." I put an arm around each of them and said, "Don't ever change."

My folks may have been unconventional, some would say rather outlandish at times with their obsession with nineteen-fifties music and fashion, but they were loving, caring, trustworthy, and kind people who had broken with convention and gone their own way in life.

They didn't do what everyone else did and never had. They lived the lives they wanted to and truly didn't care what anyone else thought. I admired them immensely for that, and it meant I had grown up with a strong belief in myself and my own abilities and had forged my own path in life. Yes, I also blew up that path with a heavy duty emotional bomb, but that was my fault entirely. Now I was back doing what I should have done many years ago, and it was thanks to them and their advice as I grew up. I would always be grateful.

"What's he grinning at us like that for?" Dad asked Mum.

"He loves us," said Mum, smiling happily.

"I do. Now, let's see if you two can help solve this case, shall we?"

"I already told you both I helped with the last one," protested Dad.

"Dad, you didn't. I figured out who it was and what happened. You might have given moral support, and it was great spending time with you, but that's not solving a case. Show me what you're made of this time."

"I will." Dad turned serious, nodded, then began inspecting every square inch of the parapet, walls, and floor, determined to uncover something worthwhile.

Mum and I did the same, and although my uncle and I had performed this task already, for some reason I was certain Dad's insistence on re-examining the scene was the right call. While they searched, I led Anxious over to where the crisp packet had been and let him have a good sniff. I then offered a biscuit in return for anything he might uncover, and he was only too keen to oblige.

Although he'd gone over the scene earlier, this time he was much more thorough, and that was my fault, not his. I hadn't focused on the litter, believing it to be just that. Anxious made a circuit, nose to the ground, but it turned out that Dad's nose was just as good and he shouted, "I've got something," then leaned right into one of the arches and pulled back with something grasped tightly in his hand.

"What is it?" I asked, hurrying over with the others.

"Just a sweet wrapper by the looks of it," he said, disappointment evident.

"For chocolate eclairs," I said, recognising the blue wrapper.

"Ooh, they're lovely. Can we get some?" asked Mum.

"Maybe later?" I suggested. "The weddings will start soon."

"Wonder if this is a clue?" asked Dad. As he heaved on the wall to stand, he released the wrapper and it sailed away on the breeze, lost to the trees or the river. "I guess we won't be getting that tested for fingerprints," he laughed.

"I don't think they can test things that small," I said, wondering if it had been important but doubting it was.

I gave Anxious a treat as he'd worked hard, then we spent a few more minutes checking things over, everyone agreeing that it would be easy to shove Neil from behind without anyone seeing, but only if his lower legs were pushed. That wasn't how it had appeared from below, so I was still uncertain how it was accomplished.

"Dad, how much do you know about Freya?"

"Not much. Ernie raved about her the moment they got together, but we've only met her a few times. She's a sweet girl."

"She's a woman in her fifties. Hardly a girl."

"You know what I mean. She's nice. Good for him. It's very sudden, but I get it. He's been on his own a long time, so deserves to be happy. Why? What are you thinking?"

"He's wondering if it could have been Freya getting rid of Neil."

"No, it's nothing like that. I'm just making sure Ernie's done the right thing. I'm sure he has, but I just wondered. Have you met her friend, Rachel? Her dog, Two-tone, is marrying Special, Freya's Lab later, and I spoke to her earlier. Apparently, she knew all about Neil and his ways, which is another person who didn't think much of him."

"We haven't met her. I'm sure your uncle knows what he's doing. He's a smart guy. Takes after his brother. Do you suspect this friend?"

"Not really, but she was worried about Freya not being around as much once she was married. And I heard she was upset because she was excluded from the sisters' business. Something seemed off about the whole thing, but I don't know if that's me picking up on the vibe, feeling a little disappointment, or it's something else."

"So now we have three suspects," declared Mum, rubbing her hands together. "Freya, her sister, or this Rachel."

"Involved, yes, but there are plenty of other suspects here too. I hadn't realised how cutthroat the whole dog wedding thing is. Everyone vying for the best spot, arguing over minor details, and there was this man, Marcus, who wasn't happy with things at all. Apparently, he's caused a lot of trouble over the years."

"What's that got to do with killing Neil?" asked Dad.

"Probably nothing, but I'm just saying there are people here who aren't too happy with how things are run. They all have their own agenda. Could be any one of them, or somebody else entirely who has nothing to do with the weddings. Neil and Marcus worked together, and apparently they revelled in forcing small businesses to fold.

They'd find ways to shut them down so big companies didn't have the competition. Nasty stuff."

"I bet it was someone you've already met," said Dad, nodding vigorously. "They always hang around to gloat and rub your nose in it."

"That absolutely doesn't always happen. I think we should go down now. They'll be doing the dog weddings and I promised I'd be there. I hope it doesn't take too long. I'm starving and looking forward to the party afterwards. I also want to change back into my usual gear."

"You look very smart," said Mum, adjusting my braces like I was a small boy. "Better than your ratty jeans and those awful Crocs. Your hair's grown again, too, and that beard is beginning to give me angry looks. I think it's become sentient."

"It might need a slight trim," I admitted. "Let's get some shade. The stone reflects the heat so much I can't stand it."

We descended into the interior of the building and remained in the shade for a while to cool down, watching everyone prepare for what to them was the main event. Plenty had the same idea as us so were sheltering by the walls to keep themselves and their animals fresh. Judging by the amount of hairspray and products they were using to pimp up their pets, it was a good job, too, as I doubted they'd last long in the sun without combusting.

"Look at these numpties," scoffed Dad, shaking his head.

"Jack, you take that back," ordered Mum.

"I will not. Marriage is a sacred vow to declare your love and your promise to cherish the other person. This makes a mockery of it."

"That's because you're looking at it all wrong," said Mum calmly, surprising us both with her sincerity.

"How so, love?" asked Dad, as intrigued as me.

"People love their pets, right?" We agreed they did. "And they want the best for them?" We nodded. "And everyone loves a wedding." Dad and I exchanged a look, as we'd been to some right stinkers and it always ended up with someone falling over drunk on the dance floor, or a speech dredging up family feuds from decades ago that left the wedding parties in two halves and nobody talking to each other.

"Not always," I ventured.

"Course they do," said Mum brightly. "The chance to wear a new hat, get dressed up, be part of a happy day. Some of these people like to relive that. They want the fun of it, but as they aren't getting hitched themselves this is their way of being the focus of the wedding but also including their beloved dogs. It's fun, and that's what life's about."

"Maybe, but it's still not right. Marriage is for those who know what they are agreeing to. For people," said Dad.

"Jack, stop being so grumpy. It's a bit of fun. An excuse to have a party. Yes, it's so others will admire the dogs that have been pampered, but there's no harm in it. I think it's sweet."

"Nothing sweet about that," countered Dad, pointing at a small group crowded around a snow-white Poodle that looked ready to bolt at any second. "Look at them. They're backcombing the poor thing's fur. It clearly isn't happy, and it looks stupid."

"Don't be so judgemental. You just watch." Mum folded her arms smugly and we focused on the people pampering the confused dog. They sprayed, they combed, they adjusted the little veil, and then tied a red ribbon on for good luck, as though they thought the dog was underdressed. They stood back, beamed at one another, then the startled dog ran circles around the laughing group, jumping and barking, clearly happy and excited.

"See? I told you. The dogs that are dressed up are ones that enjoy it."

"How would you know?" asked Dad.

"Because I do."

That put an end to the conversation, and we were literally saved by the bell as it rang. Freya announced that the weddings would begin in five minutes and asked everyone to take their seats.

"I think we better go find Uncle Ernie and see if we're needed for anything," I suggested.

"Yes, let's," said Dad hurriedly. "He'll most likely want a hand celebrating at the bar while this happens. I suppose I better oblige."

"I'll check with Freya and see if I can help," pouted Mum.

"I'll come with you, Dad," I said with a wink.

We trailed behind the keen owners and not always as keen dogs, mostly as they had no idea what was happening, then split up and did indeed find Uncle Ernie at the bar sipping on a glass of wine.

"Congratulations again," said Dad. "Sorry we blew it and got here late. I really wanted to see you get married."

"Don't worry about it," said Uncle Ernie, eyes focused on Freya as she ascended the steps and stood in the doorway with Susie, ready to perform the wedding vows for the marriages.

"You really love her, don't you?" asked Dad.

"Of course I do. I wouldn't marry her otherwise. I'm shattered though. Too much stress, and too much drama. That damn Neil. Why'd he have to die today of all days?"

"Very inconsiderate," agreed Dad. "The killer could have struck on a less important day."

"True," agreed Uncle Ernie.

I looked from one to the other, but they were both serious, and it was at times like this that I had to remind myself that sometimes my family were rather odd. In a good way, of course, but odd nevertheless.

"How's Susie taking it now?" I asked. "I'm surprised she's so involved. Didn't she want to leave Freya to take control of things?"

"She said that was unfair as it's her big day, but I don't think she's that bothered. Sure, there have been lots of tears, but deep down she's relieved he's gone."

"Was she pretending to be upset then?" asked Dad.

Uncle Ernie shrugged. "Don't think so. It was a real shock, obviously, but he wasn't exactly the love of her life. Just a mean man who liked to bully others. She's got over it quickly, so that tells you all you need to know, I guess."

"Bet she did it then," said Dad, blunt as always.

"Jack, don't be daft. She's not about to kill her husband on a day like this. She wouldn't do that to Freya."

"Then maybe it was an accident," mumbled Dad, looking disappointed.

"No way. You didn't know him. The guy absolutely wouldn't do this. Something's up and we need to figure it out. For Freya and for Susie. This is their reputation, and Neil dying is bad for their company."

"In the short term, but at least now she can control her business how she wants without him interfering," I said.

"True, but I'm telling you, it wasn't her. You'd have to be an expert climber to get up and down so fast without anyone noticing."

"Or a gymnast," I said, my focus lingering on Rachel as she led Two-tone up the steps then paused beside Special and Freya.

"You think it might be Rachel?" asked Uncle Ernie.

"She's miffed she wasn't part of the business, worried Freya will ditch her for you, and maybe she had an issue with Neil."

"So did plenty of people. Especially Marcus," said Uncle Ernie.

Our eyes drifted to Marcus who was making a very loud fuss of his dog, almost drowning out Susie's words as she began the ceremony for the two best friends and their dogs.

"He is bitter about the whole arrangement, and had an argument with Neil, apparently, but why kill him?" I asked.

"Spite? Easy pickings? To get his own back on Susie? Could be any number of reasons."

"I think you're both wrong. I know I'm not quite up-to-speed with everything yet, but if I had to guess, I reckon it's a motive you haven't even thought of yet. Sure, Susie has recovered from the shock, but if she didn't even like her own husband that's understandable. We need to keep looking, and the truth will come out."

We nodded our agreement. Dad was right. The true culprit was yet to reveal themselves and we had to find the real motive.

Chapter 9

Two-tone and Special behaved impeccably and sat on the steps, dressed to the nines, while Susie read the vows. Freya was still resplendent in her wedding clothes, with Rachel a clone of her best friend. Susie had changed into regular but smart clothes so as not to confuse everyone, including the dogs, and wore a fresh, yellow summery dress with a short hem and no sleeves, showing off toned arms and a deep tan.

The vows were rather unconventional, mostly about promising to share biscuits and not take up the entire seat on trips in the car, but once they were pronounced married there was a generous round of applause and the couple headed over to the table under the marquee where the certificates were handed out.

Freya had to hurry back to help with the rest of the vows, leaving Rachel alone with the dogs. Her smile faded as she watched Freya go, and I wondered if it was merely sadness that her best friend was now married, or something else was behind her dour expression.

There was little time to dwell on such matters, though, as the next group was already ascending the steps and the ceremony underway. In five minutes it was all over, and as the pet-friendly confetti was thrown and the inevitable chaos ensued, the line at the marquee soon became long as the wedding planners read the various scripts agreed on by the owners. Dog couples bounded down the aisle, the smiling faces making me change my mind about how important this was to everyone involved.

Anxious watched with a curious fascination, head cocked, but he remained aloof, only going over to congratulate Special and Two-tone, have a little play, then return to us and continue watching as though he understood this was more for show than anything, but intrigued nevertheless.

"What do you reckon, Anxious? Is there a special someone in your life who you'd like to marry one day?"

The little guy barked, his ears bouncing as he locked eyes on my pocket. For a moment I thought he wanted biscuits, but then realised he was fixed on where my phone was.

"You mean Min, don't you? Aw, you miss her too?"

A bark in the affirmative, focus still on my pocket.

"I'm sorry, but she's away and we can't call her. We both promised no contact, just for a week. She'll be back in no time. But I have to tell you that if anyone's going to marry Min, it will be me. You're more like our son than, er, whatever it would be if you married her."

"Complicated. That's what it would be," laughed Dad.

"It sure would," I agreed.

"Look at this bloke. What's he up to?"

"That's Marcus, the guy who's been causing bother. He fell out with Neil and just about everyone else."

"Why does he keep sliding over to the left like that?"

"Because he insists he's trained his dog to do tricks from only one side and got really shirty when he was told he had to stand on the right."

"That's dumb."

Uncle Ernie, Dad, Anxious, and I watched in morbid fascination as Marcus and his dog, Buttercup, edged further and further across to the left in a weird shuffle I was certain he believed nobody noticed. Patrick, the owner of Buttercup's betrothed, hissed something, his face reddening, but Marcus continued his peculiar sidestep.

Freya and Susie exchanged a worried look, then Freya interrupted the vows she was giving and that the owners repeated for their dogs, and bent and spoke quietly to Marcus.

He shook his head, flung his arms up, but nevertheless eased back to the correct position.

Freya continued, then Marcus clearly believed he had to show off what Buttercup had been taught so squatted and whispered to him, then stood tall, faced the crowd, and with his index finger made a circle.

Taking his cue, Buttercup leaped high, or high for him, somersaulted, and landed.

Or he would have if they'd been on the opposite side, but he landed not on Marcus' left as they'd practised, but his right, and was thrown off balance by clipping the edge of the next step up, and lost his footing. Buttercup toppled over the side backwards, and landed with a whimper on the compact ground four feet below.

For an average-sized dog this might not have been an issue, but Buttercup was smaller than a single step and was howling in pain.

Marcus roared, "My darling Buttercup," hissed at Patrick, Freya, and Susie, then raced down the steps and over to the bewildered dog. He scooped him up in his arms and sat, clutching the poor thing tight and sobbing into his shaking fur.

The assembled guests shouted questions or ridiculed Marcus for being so stubborn and risking his supposed beloved friend. Dogs barked in sympathy for Buttercup as Freya, Susie, and Patrick hurried to help.

"Stay out of this one, Son," warned Dad with a hand to my shoulder. "You too, Ernie. Let the professionals deal with this."

"You're right. We'll only be in the way. What was he thinking trying to get Buttercup to do a trick when it was so dangerous?"

"He's a stubborn guy," noted Uncle Ernie. "Freya's spoken about him quite often and he's always the same. Interfering, and always got an opinion. But the poor guy must feel awful. This was his big day after years of waiting, and now he's blown it. He'll be mortified and so upset about the accident. Everyone's making fun of him, which isn't nice. But that's what happens when you try to act superior."

"And that's something both he and Neil have in common," I noted, not knowing if it was important or not.

"Blimey, it's getting out of hand now," said Dad.

A group of owners had crowded around and were shouting at Marcus for being so stupid and endangering his dog like that. Most seemed more concerned with the delay it caused to their own weddings and that he'd scared the dogs who, rightly so, were now wary of the steps.

Marcus stood, and with Buttercup in his arms he ran up the steps, turned to the crowd, and shouted, "Don't you make fun of me. I've waited so long for our special day and now you people have ruined it. It's just awful. I'm mortified. All my plans ruined. Buttercup's fine, and that's the only good thing to come out of this terrible day." With that, he turned and raced through the doorway into the interior, his sobs echoing off the walls before all that was left was shocked silence then murmurs of sympathy and apologies that maybe they shouldn't have been so mean to a clearly sensitive soul.

"Maybe these things aren't so bad after all," said Dad cheerily as he nabbed a second glass of fizz from the bar and sipped happily.

"These people are crazy," whined Mum as she snatched Dad's drink from his raised hand and finished it in a single gulp.

"Hey, that was mine!"

"Get another one. It's free anyway." Mum smiled to show Dad she was being playful, so he took two more drinks and handed her another, taking her empty glass. "Thanks, love, and sorry to be grumpy."

"Think nothing of it," said Dad happily. "What's wrong?"

"That Marcus bloke is a very strange person." Mum shook her head, then gulped her wine.

"He must be, if you think he's strange," laughed Dad.

"What's that supposed to mean?" Mum lowered her drink and fixed him with the "I dare you" stare. He dared not, and found everything but the love of his life suddenly very interesting.

"Did you speak to him?" I asked.

"Just then. I told Freya I'd try to calm him down, but he was very rude and blamed Freya and Susie for ruining everything. He's not very happy with the man whose dog his was marrying. I've changed my mind about this whole business. Whoever heard of such a thing? Dogs can't get married. They won't be able to keep a ring on." Mum nodded sagely, like her words were wise rather than worrying; we remained quiet.

"Now what's happening?" asked Uncle Ernie, turning at the commotion.

Dogs were racing around the aisles, confused by the shouting and Marcus' angry outburst, the owners adding to the problem by arguing with each other about whose turn it was to get married next and if Marcus should be allowed to have another ceremony.

When Buttercup burst through the entrance and howled as if in real pain, the entire site suddenly went quiet and everyone focused on the tiny Chihuahua yipping incessantly. A chill ran down my spine and I told Uncle Ernie, "Something's about to happen. Buttercup's warning us. Come on."

I raced after Anxious who was already running towards the steps. Uncle Ernie, Mum, and Dad were by my side, then Uncle Ernie steamed ahead, launched up the steps, and we gave chase after a retreating Buttercup and hurried into the interior. Buttercup was at the far end where the building was less accessible, barking as he looked up at the high wall and the arches over the parapet.

High up on one corner, Marcus teetered, raised his hand to shield his eyes like Neil had done, then staggered forward and plummeted.

"Don't look," I warned Mum just in time and spun her quickly as I heard the thud of Marcus hitting the ground.

Buttercup howled, his pitiful cry ringing in my ears. Anxious joined him, expressing sympathy for the loss, the call picked up by the numerous dogs now streaming into the palace interior until it was like an overrun dog compound.

"Why does this keep happening?" gasped Uncle Ernie.

"That bloke just stepped out into nothing." Dad frowned, eyes on me, then turned back to the grisly scene.

"You don't need to protect me," whispered Mum, then we stared at the broken body of poor Marcus.

"I didn't want you to see," I explained, putting my arm around her. She trembled, but then went rigid; Mum was a fighter and refused to let things overwhelm her.

"You're such a sweet boy. Why would he jump? Just because the wedding went wrong? It makes no sense."

"It really doesn't," I agreed. "Uncle Ernie, did you see anyone else?"

"What?" He tore his eyes from Marcus, rubbed them vigorously, then focused on me. "Um, no, nothing. Did anyone else see anything? Why are people jumping off walls on my wedding day? It's starting to annoy me."

"I bet it is," chirped Dad, slapping his brother on the back. "Maybe you're cursed," he teased. When nobody spoke, Dad's smile faded. "Sorry. The stress got to me. Ernie, that was awful. But this can't be a coincidence, can it? I mean, one suicide is terrible, but two? That doesn't make any sense whatsoever."

"No, it doesn't. Max, you have to help us out here. Poor Freya will be beside herself. There's something weird going on and you have to figure it out."

"I'm trying my best."

"Don't worry," said Mum brightly. "We're here now, so between us, I'm sure we'll get this solved before the big party tonight. Are we still on for the afternoon buffet? I'm starving. How much longer will the weddings take?"

My mouth opened and closed, but no words would emerge. Even though I knew her so well, sometimes my mother still managed to shock me.

"Love, I don't think there will be a party," said Dad.

"There absolutely will," grunted Uncle Ernie, jaw clenched. "Nobody is going to ruin my big day. Nobody."

"That's the spirit," beamed Mum.

I left them to it and hurried over to Marcus, already surrounded by a sea of concerned people. I kept one eye on him, one on the wall where he'd jumped from, and skirted the crowd then checked out the other side, but there was nobody and nothing there.

Returning to Marcus, I bent beside Patrick who had his ear to his chest. He leaned back and declared, "He's dead," with a sob, tears rolling down his cheeks.

"I'm so sorry," I said.

"I may as well have pushed him. It's my fault. He killed himself because he couldn't stand the shame. I'm to blame."

"It's not your fault. He was upset, but that wasn't your doing. Come on, let's move away." I helped Patrick stand, then led him away as more people came to see what had happened. I spotted Freya, Susie, and Rachel together at the entrance, then they rushed over to us.

"Is it true?" asked Susie, glancing past me to the press of bodies obscuring Marcus from view. "Did he jump?"

"That's what it looked like," I admitted.

"Max, you have to figure this out. There is absolutely no way two suicides could happen in one day. Please, help us," wailed Susie, tears streaming.

"We just saw him jump," said Patrick, frowning. "What do you mean?"

"It's too much of a coincidence," said Rachel. "Something's going on here. That's obvious."

"Why would you say such a thing?" asked Patrick. "Everyone saw Marcus jump, and I know it's awful but Neil did the same. I can't imagine how terrible this is for you, Susie, but you have to accept the truth."

"Never! Neil was a mean-spirited, awful man, even if he was my husband, but jump? No! And poor Marcus? Yes, he was upset, but not distraught enough to take his own life."

"You mean this isn't my fault?" asked Patrick, hope in his eyes. "It's not because of what happened at the ceremony?"

"We don't think so," I said. "But nobody knows the truth, and nobody saw anything. Let's get everyone away from Marcus and leave the police to do their work. I can hear the sirens, so they'll be here soon."

Just then, the paramedics from the morning bustled through the entrance, toting heavy looking bags. Our eyes met and both raised their eyebrows at me. I shook my head as they approached.

"You got here quick," I noted.

"We've had a quiet day and were taking a break when we got the call. We were in the car park," said the man I recalled was named Peter.

"Good job too. Can you show us?" asked Amy, his partner.

"Of course." I led the way to Marcus, the guests moving aside now help was at hand, although everyone knew he was already dead. Freya and Susie began corralling guests outside and away from the terrible sight, leaving only a few people inside the grounds, and we converged on the paramedics as they bent to Marcus.

We watched as they performed their checks to confirm he had passed, then waited while they called it in and moved aside to talk in private. There seemed to be an argument as Amy hissed something, clearly angry, while Peter crossed his arms and shook his head. They both glanced our way, our group now the only ones close by.

With a final word, they returned to Marcus and Peter covered him with a blanket, almost casually. Everyone sighed with relief, the sight of him hard to look away from. The paramedics stood, exchanged a frown, then turned to us.

"Two suicides in one day at the same spot? With the same people involved?" Peter shook his head and waited for someone to speak.

"It can't be suicide," said Uncle Ernie. "No way. We had our doubts this morning, but now? No chance. It's a conspiracy."

"What other explanation is there?" asked Peter.

"Murder!" shouted Mum, her cry echoing from the walls, causing a communal gasp from the congregation who were clearly waiting just outside the various entrances.

"But I'm guessing that just like this morning, nobody noticed anything untoward and there are witnesses who saw everything?" asked Amy.

"Yes, but that doesn't matter. Someone's up to something. It's obvious."

"Not to me, it isn't," said Peter. "And this time, we won't be moving the body." His words were directed at Amy, who bristled but said nothing.

"We saw him," admitted Uncle Ernie, "but so what? That doesn't mean he, er, well, I suppose he did do it himself. But there's something going on, we all know it. There has to be."

"I'm sorry this has happened again, but I think you need to admit that when there are eyewitnesses to such terrible events, there's no conspiracy. What you saw is what happened."

"He's right," said Amy, voice full of sympathy. "We moved Neil out of consideration for you," she told Susie, "but we got into trouble. This time we have to leave the deceased where he fell, but these are obvious cases of suicide. Maybe it's because of the heightened emotions on such a big day, but if there are witnesses." Amy shrugged, leaving everyone silent, no sound but the approaching sirens of yet more police and no doubt the detective from earlier.

The paramedics packed up their gear and asked us to wait outside the palace. We reluctantly agreed, but as I turned back before we left, I noted both looking up at the wall and shaking their heads before conversing quietly. They didn't believe this was suicide either, but were clearly keeping their opinions to themselves.

Leaving the others at the doorway, I rushed back over and asked, "Is there any way to make someone jump? Have you ever had anything like this happen before?"

"Nothing that I know of," said Amy.

"Nor me. And no, nothing like this has ever happened before. This is very weird, bordering on suspicious, but that's not for us to say. We help people, but aren't the police. Sorry, but there's nothing we can do."

I thanked them then returned to the others, but something about Peter's attitude gave me pause. He clearly wasn't happy about what Amy had said. Maybe she didn't believe it was suicide, or maybe he was as confused as the rest of us.

Chapter 10

Anxious was actually anxious. As we emerged into the blistering sunshine from the shady interior, the shock hit yet again. Nobody could get used to this weather, no matter how long it lasted. As we gasped, the little guy mewled and clawed gently at my legs. Not enough to hurt, but enough to make his presence known.

He whined as I bent to check on him, eyes darting to the crowds and the chaotic mess of dogs forgotten because of Marcus' demise.

"A bit too much for you, is it?" I asked my best buddy.

Anxious barked his agreement, his small body trembling as he tried to hold it together.

"Let's get him away from here," said Dad kindly.

"We'll go and look at the cathedral," suggested Mum. "Sit on the grass and calm down."

"Good idea. Thanks, guys. Anxious, would you like that? Just the four of us somewhere else?"

A bark in the affirmative, then he jumped into my arms and I stood, cradling his warm body. He slowly calmed, the shaking subsiding, so we said our goodbyes before heading off to the cathedral.

"It's like a different world over here," noted Dad as we settled on a grassy bank under the shade of a willow.

"Like none of that craziness is going on a few minutes away." Mum stroked Anxious where he was sprawled out, wedged between her and Dad, comforted by their presence when so much else was unfamiliar. "How do you do this, Max?" she asked, adding a tut for good measure.

"It's nothing to do with me. I think we all know this is tied up with Vee. She's a van on a mission to right the wrongs in this country, and I think I'm just along for the ride."

"You don't still believe that, do you?" asked Dad, adjusting his fat turn-ups and rolling his T-shirt sleeves up to reveal more biceps.

"I do. Ever since this first started, I encounter one mystery after another. It's definitely to do with the van. It's like a mystery-mobile. Righting wrongs, ensuring I stay busy and occupied to keep me from ever questioning if I made the right choice leaving everything to roam around."

"And did you?" asked Dad with a smirk.

"Absolutely. This is the right decision, and I'm never going back to how things were."

"Good lad. But I don't think it's the campervan. That old VW is just a vehicle. It's you, not her."

"It is the van," said Mum. "It's Max, Anxious, and the van. Not just them, but us too. And Min. We're in this together. A family. I know it's our Max who solves most of the crimes, but don't you understand?" she asked Dad.

"Enlighten me."

"We're the backbone to what he does. His support. The reason he does it. We help, but not just by figuring things out. By being there when he needs us, and even when he doesn't." Mum paused to laugh and smile at me. "And something about Vee makes it happen."

"That's not like you, love." Dad squeezed her hand and added, "You always say stuff like that is hippy nonsense."

"And just this once, I've been proven wrong."

We almost choked, and ended up coughing as we tried to speak, but what words were there for the woman who, according to her, and nobody would ever argue, had never before been wrong about anything in her entire life?

"So what do we make of this?" asked Mum, trying to hide her broad grin and failing. "It's an awful thing to happen on what's meant to be a happy day. Poor Ernie and Freya. Could somebody be doing it to ruin their lovely day?"

"It's an extreme way to do it," said Dad. "And besides, they got married already. Why kill that weird bloke, Marcus, when the marriage was a done deal?"

"To make everyone unhappy." Mum stroked Anxious who was now fast asleep, then brightened and said, "Maybe it's a rival business. I bet there aren't that many dog wedding planners, so it's probably that. Another company getting rid of the competition. It might ruin their reputation and they'll be bankrupt."

"We would have seen them here, surely?" I said. "Nobody's mentioned another company."

"Oh, what about the wife? Bet she did it as she hated her husband."

"It's a possibility, but she's a great actor if it was her. And why do it today of all days, and in such a weird way? She'd be risking everything, like you said."

"Do we trust Freya?" asked Mum.

"Mum, you can't say that!"

"He's right, love. Freya's a lovely woman and we both like her. No way would she do this? Although, maybe she did it to get her sister away from Neil."

"Guys, there's one glaring issue. Why Marcus too? What did he have to do with it? All we have to go on is that

Neil was a bad husband and Marcus was a busybody and annoying. He was upset about the ceremony being ruined, and next thing we know he's dead. What we really need to figure out is how do you make it look like suicide if it's murder? I mean, I saw both of them fall."

"We saw it too," said Dad, deflated. "I guess there's only one answer then."

"Which is?"

"There were no murders." The disappointment in his voice was obvious, and Mum reluctantly nodded in agreement.

"That's the obvious answer, I know." I considered my words carefully, then asked, "Are we really saying we believe two men jumped from a ruin at a wedding on the same day even though everyone who knows them insists there is no way they would do such a thing? That they both decided they'd had enough and chose this day to do it?"

"But Marcus was distraught about the ruined ceremony," said Dad. "Maybe he got the idea from Neil and just lost the plot."

"This is a real head-scratcher."

"Don't worry, Son, you'll figure it out." He patted my leg, frowned when his sleeve unrolled, so hurriedly fixed it.

"I hope so. We don't want Freya and Susie going out of business because everyone believes their events are jinxed. And I have to know how this was done."

"This is one mystery he absolutely won't let lie," Dad told Mum.

"Of course he won't. I'm dying to know how it was done."

"He'll figure it out," Dad reassured her.

I zoned out as they spoke about me like I wasn't there, and noticed someone I'd have rather not spoken to approach.

Anxious growled in his sleep, clearly sensing something, and his fur bristled.

"What's got into him?" asked Mum.

"He knows who's coming." I nodded in the direction of DI Dai Davies as he huffed and puffed across the grass, ignoring the paths, eyes never still as he scanned for either us or the killer. Did he still believe Neil's death wasn't murder, or had Marcus' demise changed his mind? I also realised I hadn't been up to investigate where Marcus jumped from, but would have to check it out, no matter what the detective said.

"He looks dodgy. Is he the killer?" asked Mum, squinting as she always thought it made her look intimidating. It did.

"No, he's the detective in charge. We spoke this morning and he insisted it wasn't a crime. He wasn't happy with the paramedics for moving Neil, and he wasn't too impressed with me either. Be nice, and hopefully this won't take long. I suppose we'll need to make statements."

"He better not be mean to my boy," hissed Mum. I smiled at her and shook my head. "What?"

"I'm in my thirties. I can handle myself."

"That's not the point. I'm your mother, so will always try to protect you. It's the law of parenting."

"True," agreed Dad happily, rolling his sleeves up extra high and pumping his arms so the blood made the veins bulge.

Anxious finally woke and sat, sniffing until he found his mark. A low rumble came from deep within his chest, which was unusual for him as he never showed aggression just because he wasn't fond of someone, only when there was no other choice.

"Easy there, tiger," I warned.

"You!" spat Dai as he loomed in front of us, blocking the view of the cathedral.

"Me," I agreed happily, having learned long ago that when people are rude the best way to act is polite as it annoys them even more and they get flummoxed.

Anxious stood, wagged happily, then fixed his attention on Dai's pocket. What was with him? First growling, now happy?

"Anxious, you're being weird."

My buddy turned, licked his lips, then spun in a circle as if to show Dai how great he was, then plonked himself down and awaited his prize.

"Fine," sighed Dai, his hunched shoulders loosening as he tried to hide a smile. He pulled out a biscuit for Anxious, who took it gently, then snapped back into grumpy DI mode and glared at me.

"What's going on?" asked Dad. "Why is Anxious acting like he hates this guy then showing off?"

"Because he knows I'm in a very bad mood and picked up on it, then remembered I'm the biscuit detective," explained Dai, face serious.

"Um, right." Dad was at a loss. So was I.

"Before I even begin, I want to get one thing straight. Everyone saw Marcus jump. Everyone said he was distraught because of the failed wedding, which is beyond dumb if you ask me. I want a quick statement, then this is done."

"Fine by us," I said, smiling again.

"We were just relaxing, so that sounds perfect," said Mum.

After introductions were made, we each gave a brief statement, then Dai grunted and turned to leave.

"Wait! What happens now?" I asked.

"As before, and I can't believe I'm saying this, everyone is free to go about their business. The death was witnessed, there is nothing to be done, so guests can either stay or leave. Their choice. I believe a number of them have already left, and I don't blame them, as even for this bunch of whack jobs it's too much for one day. What is with these people? Jumping off important historic buildings and freaking everyone out? Ridiculous!"

"You're still convinced these weren't murders?" I asked, wondering if this was a ploy to stop me interfering.

"Max, there are multiple eyewitnesses, including you. This isn't a spy movie where they had implants in their brains forcing them to do things against their will. It's a group dog and human wedding, which, as far as I'm concerned, is enough to make anyone top themselves."

"Bit of a coincidence, isn't it?" insisted Mum, matching Dai's stern stare and upping him considerably.

"Lady, that means nothing."

"Don't you 'lady' my wife," warned Dad, hackles up more than Anxious facing a bear with a pack of sausages between them.

"That's right. Nobody calls me a lady," hissed mum. She frowned, considered her words, then added, "You know what I mean," and crossed her arms.

"Look, it wasn't murder! How many times do I have to say it? Yes, it's an astonishing coincidence, but everyone saw them do it. Unless they were controlled by robots, or forced somehow, then there's no other possible explanation. I looked into Neil just to satisfy myself, and came up with nothing. No sign of him being down enough to do what he did, but no enemies beyond what you'd expect from a man like him. This Marcus guy was a pain by all accounts, and not someone who made mortal enemies."

"But neither would jump either," insisted Mum.

"But they did, didn't they? I'm sorry, and this case is unusual, but sometimes these things happen."

"Do they?" I asked, trying to be nice and calm Dai down. "Do things like this really happen? Double suicides?"

"No, they don't," he sighed, wiping his forehead. "Max, if you figure it out, be sure to let me know," he chuckled, then nodded and left.

"That bloke's weird," noted Dad as we watched Dai hurry back across the grass.

"He's not the friendliest man, but then he suddenly acts nice. I don't think he's a bad guy, but I think he's wrong." I couldn't help wondering how long it would take for the scene to be cleared and how many people would want to continue with their ceremonies, if any.

"I like him," chirped Mum. "He speaks his mind, doesn't pretend to be someone he isn't, and is obviously good at his job."

"Even if he's closing these cases so fast without even considering they were murders?" I asked.

"Yes, because it's obvious to everyone but us and a few others that they were suicides. You can't blame him for that."

"What's got into you, love?" asked Dad, as concerned as me by Mum's strange act of being considerate and understanding.

"I'm trying not to judge. To give everyone more of a chance. Not to be so hasty making my mind up about strangers. That's good, right? Max has mellowed since he started vanlife, and I want to do the same."

"That's great, Mum."

"Yeah. Well done, love."

"He was a bit of a fat loser though," sighed Mum. Her hand shot to her mouth and she gasped as she realised what she'd said.

Dad and I just laughed. The woman we knew and loved was back. Blunt, honest, and unapologetic, even if sometimes I wished she would be more considerate and less judgemental.

Knowing we should return to see if there was anything we could do, we reluctantly made our way back to the palace. Police were already removing the crime scene tape and leaving, while DI Davies gave instructions to the remaining teams. I estimated that at least a third of the people had left, the stress of the day too much, and wondered if they'd be given a refund. That would be a big loss for Freya and Susie, so maybe this was a rival company doing something underhand to put them out of business.

But the same question kept surfacing.

How?

I knew there was no way I was going to discover the truth unless I just let the day play out, so vowed to see it through and remain attentive. Something would surface, I'd pick up on a clue, and gradually things would fall into place. But this time, it felt like I was up against it and denying the obvious conclusion.

Freya made an announcement from the top of the steps, explaining that the ceremonies would go ahead and the police had given her permission. A cheer rang out, shocking me, but those who remained were smiling and happy with the news, which I found incredible.

The remaining weddings began to take place, Freya and Susie professional and patient with the owners and dogs, and everything ran smoothly. Mum and Dad scoffed and sniggered the whole time, getting plenty of dirty looks from the owners, but, as usual, they were oblivious to everything going on around them. I suspected, like always, that it wasn't so much they didn't see or hear it, but they simply didn't care. Their confidence was always astonishing to me growing up. How they could dress the way they did, act how they did, and not care what anyone else thought, but it was also truly inspiring.

They were comfortable in their own skins and refused to bow to convention, and I supposed I had finally followed in their footsteps and jumped off the daily grind of work and always striving for more and finally gone my own way. Defying what a recently divorced man was meant to do, and swapping it for a much freer, and certainly more interesting life.

"Uncle Ernie, how are they doing?" I asked as he joined us at the bar.

"Pretty good. Most of those who left had already had their ceremonies, so were leaving anyway. Not everyone was planning on staying for the buffet and party tonight. That's more about our wedding than theirs anyway. The girls are relieved as they've still managed to cover the costs, but it's got them worried about the future."

"They'll be fine," said Dad. "Give it a few weeks and people will have forgotten. And besides, others won't even know any of this happened."

"I hope you're right. Freya and Susie worked so hard to build up this business. I'd hate for it to all be for nothing."

"You wait and see. Freya's a fighter like you, Ernie. She won't let this stop her." Dad draped an arm over his brother's shoulder and smiled at him.

"Thanks, Jack. I'm glad you came."

"You're my brother. Wouldn't miss it for the world. Sorry we missed the wedding, but we're here now and have a hotel booked for tonight."

"That reminds me," I realised. "I need to find a campsite or a pitch somewhere. We'll stay for a few days and see the sights, but I need to get everything sorted. I could do with a few hours alone too. Anxious needs it even more. He's overwhelmed."

"I've been asking around, and have the perfect place for you," said Uncle Ernie.

"You do? Great. Let me have the details and I'll head off and get everything set up."

Uncle Ernie gave me directions, so with the ceremonies almost over and Freya announcing that the buffet would open in an hour, I decided to go and find the campsite and get some distance from this truly weird bunch of people and hopefully clear my head.

Chapter 11

Once again, it was like coming home as we approached Vee. Now late afternoon, the car park was at its peak with vehicles jammed in as tightly as possible. An endless stream of people drove around in circles, waiting to pounce when a space became available.

As I opened up, a man in an eighties matt black VW campervan pulled to a stop and called out, "You leaving?"

"Give me a minute, then it's yours." I gave him a thumbs up and there was an awkward moment of silence as we each eyed the other's vehicle, the admiration clear.

He burst out laughing, so did I, and he said, "Cheers, mate. That a 67 splitty? Sweet. Original interior?"

"Nearly all original, and yes, a 67. I love the paint job of yours. How does it drive?"

"Mate, it drives like an absolute nightmare," he chuckled. "Dodgy suspension, although the brakes are good, the steering is heavy, she veers like a drunken teen with a free bottle of vodka, and the damn vents pump out nothing but hot air. They're basically just holes."

"And you love it, right?" I said knowingly.

"More than any vehicle I have ever owned. Hey, you a lifer?" Like me, he had long brown hair, but unlike me he was stocky and just had stubble. Crow's feet around his brown eyes indicated this man liked to laugh.

"Vanlifer full time," I confirmed. "It's only been a few months, but it's been a revelation. I love it."

"Been over a year for me. Stick with it. The rewards are worth it."

We turned when someone beeped, so I waved to them and apologised, then told the man, "I better get going. Nice to meet you."

"You too, mate. Maybe see you around. Thanks for the spot."

"No problem."

I hurried into Vee, buckled up, then shifted forward so he could park. I checked in my mirror that he'd managed to get the space, then exited the car park and drove the short distance to the campsite Uncle Ernie had suggested. I estimated it was less than a ten-minute walk into town, so could easily leave Vee there, but I also had plans for today that I wanted to fit in, just to have some time alone, so would drive back in once we were settled at the campsite and that way we could go straight to the party later on too.

Pulling off the main road, I bounced along a track, stopped at the farm gate, did the usual of opening and closing, then parked at reception. I could already tell that this would be a perfect location, and felt butterflies as I anticipated staying somewhere so beautiful, but not quite knowing what to expect.

This was what I truly adored about vanlife. I had both the familiar and the new everywhere I went. My home had all I needed, or at least could make do with, and I knew every square inch of it intimately, but each new place I stayed had endless things of interest and I could never tire of visiting all the country had to offer. Yes, some stays were basic and uninspiring, but even they were beautiful in their own way, even if just because it was a struggle. But most sites I chose had been stunning, fun, and I would visit them again at some point.

After booking in for three nights, and assured I could stay for longer if I chose, I thanked the owner then navigated a gravel track, the ground either side worryingly bumpy, the grass overgrown and very wild. Dense thickets of gnarled trees formed a dark backdrop to the site, protecting it from the road and several fields, but leaving it open to the sea.

Turning a corner, I was greeted with the stunning vista of the placid water stretching to the horizon. I could trace the coast along to the north, but the view to the south was hidden by more trees and the natural lay of the land. My concerns about the terrain were unfounded as I noted the first of the pitches. Each was its own little private paradise surrounded by untamed, wild countryside, but with neatly mowed paths or spaces large enough for vehicles, depending on what people preferred.

I took another turn, drove up a rather steep rise, then levelled out and found my pitch.

I couldn't get out fast enough. Neither could Anxious.

"What do you think of this then?" I asked my buddy who was sitting and wagging, waiting to be told he could explore.

Anxious barked his approval, so I left him to investigate while I soaked up the utter majesty of this hidden gem of a campsite. As the owner explained, there was no electrical hook-up, and nothing different about a pitch for a campervan than a regular one, but that was what made it perfect. Whereas some sites had gravel hardstanding for vehicles, I always preferred to be on grass. It was more natural, and nothing could beat wiggling your toes in the grass on a warm day.

Behind me was the forest, dark and brooding, but with the benefit of it keeping the temperature a few degrees cooler. On either side, sturdy grass and wild plants were left to their own devices, hints of purples, blues, red, and white of the native species as beautiful as any tended garden.

Whether it was natural, or manmade, the way the land rose and fell at each pitch meant they were all private, and with added hedges where needed, it felt like a living, breathing house, albeit with the sky as my roof.

But what did that matter? I had my own metal-clad home and inside it was all I required to make this another perfect stay. Having fallen into a strict routine, I dared not rest yet for fear of dozing off and never getting organised, so the first thing I did was to check the prevailing wind then set up the sun shelter.

It took all of ten minutes, including pegging down the guy ropes and adjusting them, then I banged in the poles for the windbreak and set up the folding table I used as a kitchen worktop alongside it so the wind wouldn't blow out the gas when I cooked. I'd have to forego the usual one-pot wonder this evening, but would make up for it over the next few days, so wanted everything ready and waiting in advance.

With the table legs locked into place with the catches—a lesson I'd learned the hard way when everything collapsed early on in my vanlife endeavours—I set about unloading the hob, kettle, various plastic storage boxes containing essentials for cooking, including one for crockery and cutlery, sorted out tea towels, cloths, and a few other items, then stood back and admired my handiwork.

"Perfect," I sighed, smiling despite how often I'd performed this seemingly mundane task. I knew people laughed at this obsessive side of my nature, but when your location changed every few days, I found it to be a real sense of security, and it gave me great satisfaction to know everything was organised and I knew where things were.

With a chair set up, a blanket laid down under the sun shelter for us both, and with my large power bank still fully charged from the last place I stayed, I was fully set for a perfect few days in one of the most beautiful places I had ever visited. St Davids was definitely somewhere I would return to next year, and hopefully minus the terrible drama I'd encountered so far.

I sank into my chair gratefully, comforted by the way the material sagged and how the plastic dug into my back. Strange what a man can get used to, even crave. This chair had served me so well, and although far from a top end model, it was portable, didn't take up much room, and was part of the vanlife experience now.

I went to remove my Crocs, rather astonished to find I was still in my wedding outfit. Now feeling uncomfortable, I wondered about the etiquette for changing and decided that I absolutely could get the ska gear off and put my own clothes on. I removed my socks and wiggled my feet in the grass, then closed my eyes and smiled, letting the sun warm my face. This was the life.

Knowing I'd be asleep if I remained here, I heaved out of my chair and opened up the back of Vee then pulled out the drawer containing my limited choice of footwear.

"There you are, my beauties," I chuckled, fondling my Crocs then checking I wasn't being watched as it must look beyond weird. I put my smart shoes in the drawer then stripped down, folded the clothes, and stashed everything in the bag Uncle Ernie had given me. Back in cut-offs and a simple faded black vest, I felt like myself again and wondered how I'd cope if I had to wear a suit and tie to a job every day. Ugh. Made me shudder.

A miffed bark from the little fella made me turn, and his eyes bored into mine as he spun in a circle, reminding me that I wasn't the only one in his wedding outfit.

"I'm so sorry, buddy. Let's get that off you." Anxious lifted a paw, so I slipped the vest off his leg then repeated it for the other before pulling it over his head. "How's that?"

He did a peculiar leap into the air, more a bounce like a startled deer, then landed and ran around me several times, yipping. I had my answer.

Laughing, I opened the side door and stepped into the heart of my home. Smugness radiated as I knew I had a full water container under the sink, the grey water was empty, and the fridge was well-stocked. At least as well as it could be considering its miniature size. The food cupboards held plenty of essentials, too, even though I now kept a lot in the containers for my outdoor kitchen.

Deciding it would be fun to explore, I grabbed Anxious' lead, always an exciting moment for the keen Terrier, and after he promised to stay close, we set off for a walk around the site and to check if the approach down to the water was as thrilling as Uncle Ernie and the site owner had said.

Paths weaved this way and that, some leading to private pitches, but mostly looping around to the main gravel road that wound from top to bottom. We took our time checking things out, my eyes drawn to the incredible views of the coastline. Strange to think that Ireland wasn't far away, and then the huge Atlantic Ocean separating us from the United States.

The road petered out at a turning point where the grass was short from exposure to the elements, the soil turning to little but sand. We were still very high up, so a secure fence ensured nobody got too close to the edge. I followed the path, then read the sign warning that the way down was steep and unsuitable for anyone with qualms about heights or with limited mobility.

"What do you think? Should we take a look?"

A bark in the affirmative was the answer.

The path narrowed as it cut between thorny hedges, their stunted growth testament to the extremes of weather during the more inclement months. We took the turn and a compacted path led down the steep side of the cliff with a handrail for support. Anxious was sure-footed and unconcerned, but I wondered if Crocs were the best footwear but decided to continue and see what we discovered.

Another warning about the gradient gave me pause, especially when a thick rope replaced the handrail. I took hold of it in one hand and we descended, but the going wasn't too bad as the numerous switchbacks ensured that although we were descending a cliff it wasn't too steep to manage, even with inappropriate footwear.

I was still glad to release the rope and stand on relatively flat ground.

Anxious barked happily from his position on the rocks, the water lapping around him.

"Be careful," I warned, but this secret spot was safe enough with numerous ledges to move along the base of the cliff. The tang of salt was so strong here where the water evaporated in the pools, leaving a thick crust that baked in the sun. Mussels clung to the exposed rocks, no doubt submerged when the tide came in.

Anxious leaped from platform to platform happily, while I stood and savoured the moment. Turning back to the path, I noted something pinned to the post beside the rope. Checking we were alone, and with a shiver despite the heat, I approached, a familiar brown envelope with a string tie looped over the fastener making me certain this was from my stalker.

As if I might be unsure, my name was written on the envelope in thick marker pen, almost like a child had scrawled the words. It was fixed with a large galvanised nail, which I found more disconcerting than anything. What did that mean? I ripped the envelope free, unwound the string, and lifted the flap. The scent of aftershave made me shudder.

"Glass?" Carefully, I emptied the contents into my palm, revealing a collection of coloured glass pieces like you'd find at the beach. All were smooth and there were some intense colours, but it made no sense. First pebbles, now glass? I returned them to the envelope and noticed a slip of paper stuck to the inside, the same colour as the envelope. Mindful of anything sharp, I slid it out and unfolded it, the ragged edges signifying it had been torn from another envelope.

With my heart beating faster than I'd have liked, and my hands shaking slightly, I took several deep breaths to calm myself down, then focused on the words.

"There's no escape. I know your every move. You know why."

I absolutely did not know why. What I did know was that this was freaking me out. How had this person known I would come to this campsite and then to the sea? I hadn't even decided until we'd gone for our walk. Who knew I was here? Who knew about the secret path? Not even all the guests here would, let alone anyone else.

Only Uncle Ernie and the actual campsite owner knew I was staying here. I'd simply told Mum and Dad that I was going to a campsite. Sure, Uncle Ernie could have given them the details, and any of them might have told someone else, but what then? This mystery person hurried over, came down here, and left this cryptic message and a handful of sun-bleached, sea-washed glass?

If they wanted me so badly, why tease like this? I racked my brain trying to think if anyone who was at the wedding had been at the comedy festival where the other warnings had been given, but they absolutely hadn't. So this coward was a sneak, staying hidden? Or maybe they'd just been a face in the crowd and I wouldn't recognise them even if I did see them? Hiding in plain sight?

I didn't like this one bit. This was clearly someone with serious issues, and they were directing their anger at me in ways that gave me chills. Who leaves knives and throws pestles and mortars through windows, sneaks up on ex-wives while they sleep, and places notes to scare people? Now these little collections of glass and pebbles? Their mind was obviously unstable, and with them focusing so much on me I couldn't even imagine what they had planned.

All I could do was be cautious, but I was rattled. Was I being watched right now? Were they hiding close enough to jump out and attack me? I was getting carried away, but there was no denying they were keeping a very close eye on me to anticipate my movements so well.

After calling for Anxious, I hurried back up the path, the rope coming into its own for the arduous climb, but I wanted to see if I could spot my nemesis at the campsite as they couldn't have left the water long before we went down to explore.

It was, as expected, a lost cause, as who was I even looking for? Someone I knew from my past? A stranger? A thug hired to intimidate and scare me? It could have been any of those or something else entirely.

Deciding I would not let this get to me, and with things to do, I still sat in my chair and tried to unwind. No way would I be able to focus on the two deaths if I let this overwhelm me. And besides, there was a real corker of a puzzle to solve, and I was determined to figure out how the two men really met their grisly demise.

Chapter 12

"This is what we needed," I told my grinning buddy as we sauntered happily along the high street. "I hadn't realised how tense I was, and I can see you've relaxed too."

Anxious turned and barked as he trotted beside me, a spring in our steps, pleased to be alone.

The sheer volume of people and the chaotic day had certainly been too much for me, but I had been lax in not considering Anxious' feelings too. Like me, he was an introvert of sorts and as much as we liked people's company, we needed time alone to recover and build our energy back up. Hundreds of people and dogs, murders, and threats to my safety had combined to turn the day into both a happy and utterly stressful one.

The simple act of walking was enough to clear my head and lighten my spirits, and I could tell that Anxious was the same. There was a lightness to his movements, his little feet moving fast to keep up with my leisurely pace. Just the joy of moving and being together with space to breathe and no drama.

It also gave me time to think without being interrupted. I let the day play out in my head, not focusing on anything in particular, just seeing where it would lead. Two deaths, two apparent suicides, two perplexing people who everyone insisted would never take their own lives. What was the motive?

This was what it all boiled down to. Why make it look like suicide?

I stopped suddenly, drawn to my reflection in a shop window. Anxious sat beside me and barked as he studied us. Was this what I looked like now? I chuckled as I shook my head, my long brown hair quite wavy because of the length, my beard thick, peppered with a hint of grey that I didn't mind.

I looked so different to how I remembered myself being, as though I was a different person entirely. It wasn't just the general hippy vibe, or the extreme tan, or the way my blue eyes sparkled with a green intensity. It was something else. What had changed?

"I'm not stressed out," I told myself. It had crept up on me gradually over the months, and although I was more relaxed than I'd ever been in my life, I hadn't truly understood until this moment how utterly different I was as a person now. I'd tried my best to put my obsessive, workaholic nature behind me and to enjoy the present, not dwell on the past, but vanlife and the open road truly had been transformative.

Keeping track of personal changes like this wasn't easy, and it was seeing myself as if for the first time that made it hit home. I'd genuinely achieved what I set out to do. Put the old me behind me and embrace what had always been lurking inside. Someone who appreciated their life, what they had, and took the time to relish it. Sure, I was still the same me to some extent, but I'd managed to let go of so much and had gained so much more in the process.

Free, that's what I felt. Truly free. It wasn't just that I was a traveller now, it was because I'd relinquished not only a home but a way of life, and begun a new one. Had it really taken me blowing up my whole existence for me to become who I was now? I guess it had.

I saluted my reflection and smiled, the act triggering something in my head. Neil and Marcus had saluted before they jumped, hadn't they? I'd thought both men were shielding their eyes from the sun, but wasn't it more like a salute? Why would they do that? What did it mean? This was important. A military connection possibly?

Knowing better than to push this clue too far, I left it stewing in my subconscious as we resumed our stroll along the street busy with tourists keen to buy souvenirs or get emergency supplies for their trip.

We found the fishing shop and I bought a new reel and line, a few lures the helpful man recommended for catching mackerel, and was even given insider knowledge on the best locations away from the tourists, although I did wonder if he told everyone the same thing and I'd find myself fishing with a dozen others who believed they had a secret spot.

Back at Vee, I arranged everything, and put a bag of ice in my coolbox. I was tempted to head off on foot, keen to stretch my legs and enjoy the day rather than suffer the heat of the van which was stifling as Vee had been in the sun all day, but eventually decided to drive so I didn't have to carry everything too far. As we left the crowded streets behind and approached the coast, we sniffed as the salty tang of the sea hit. Five minutes later, we arrived in a secluded area and I parked, amazed there was nobody about.

Gulls screeched and the wind picked up as we made our way down a narrow path through gorse and dark grasses able to cope in the harsh coastal environment, then emerged into the open with the cliff edge right there.

I gasped as the sun bounced off the still water, the intensity enough to make my eyes stream. It was a truly beautiful sight, the freedom it represented reflected in my own high spirits. Boats bobbed on the water, tiny little white toys far out to sea. We turned right and followed the coastal path, then slowly weaved down the steep slope where steps had been carved roughly into the rock, worn smooth by time.

Anxious was in his element, nose to the ground, skipping over the rocks expertly, never once missing his footing. What he was tracking was anyone's guess, crabs maybe, but he was enjoying himself and that was all that mattered. Taking a sharp bend around a large outcropping, I cheered as I emerged onto a flat ledge ten feet about the water.

"Guess that guy was telling the truth," I said happily, buoyed to find we were alone in a truly isolated fishing spot.

Anxious yipped his delight then moved back into the shade of the overhanging cliffs, put his back to the wall, and curled up for a doze. Poor guy was shattered, and as I watched him settle, a deep lethargy overtook me, too, and I could hardly keep awake as I set up my gear for some light fishing.

Although no expert, I'd fished with Dad when a boy before the allure and mystery of girls and hanging with my mates took precedence. Since then, I'd let it slide, but whenever I had gone fishing I'd vowed to do it more, but life always seemed to get in the way. Options were limited as I'd never been one of those guys who was happy to fish then release their catch. For me, that seemed worse than eating what I caught, and I intended to eat the mackerel if I did manage to snag anything.

The water was so still it felt criminal to break the surface, but I cast off then watched intently as I slowly reeled the line back in. Over and over, I cast and hoped for the best, but either I was too rusty, the lures were wrong, or this wasn't a good spot. Maybe it was the heat? Maybe the fish were cooling down in the depths, not near the surface? Did fish overheat in the UK?

A tug at the line, my heart racing, I reeled in carefully, neither too fast nor too slow, and whooped as I pulled out a string of five fish on the various hooks.

Anxious woke to the noise of me packing the fish in the coolbox, and I was glad I'd brought it now—another bonus for the man in the fishing shop who'd recommended I take one. Intrigued, he joined me at the edge of the ledge as I cast off again and reeled in another three fish within minutes. He barked happily as I stored them then settled, the novelty having worn off, while I spent the next half hour catching more fish than I had imagined possible.

Rather dazed by the whole experience, I decided to call it a day as not only was I overheating but my energy levels had dipped low from the exertion. I had to remind myself that it had been a very long day with an early start, and although it was wonderful that Uncle Ernie was now a married man, it hadn't exactly been a chilled wedding.

With the coolbox full, I sat on it and leaned back against the shaded rock, pleased with my efforts, rather amazed by the quality of the fishing. Anxious stirred beside me then barked a warning. I turned to find a man approaching, and I recognised him but couldn't place where from.

"Hey," he said with a nod. "Mind if I join you in the shade for a moment? That's one steep climb down and I'm regretting it already."

"Sure. It's nice and cool over here."

He dropped his own smaller coolbox and sat on it, leaning back and sighing as the stone worked its magic and his redness receded. "Wow, that feels so nice. I love this place, but it's one helluva climb back up. I'm surprised you know about it. You're from the wedding, aren't you?"

"Ah, that's how I know you. You were there this morning then again earlier, right? I didn't recognise you out of uniform. Peter, isn't it?"

"Yeah, that's right. And you're Max. The groom's nephew, if I remember right. Terrible business today. I'm amazed he still got hitched after what happened this morning."

"They didn't want to let everyone down, and were determined to get married. Ernie's a positive guy and doesn't let things bother him too much, but it wasn't the best start to a wedding."

Anxious shuffled over for a fuss, but his heart wasn't in it and when Peter didn't react right away he just grumbled and curled up between the coolboxes.

"Good for him. I'm assuming the actual wedding went okay?" Peter pulled out a handkerchief and wiped his face, the sweat slick on his forehead. "Man, I'm so hot. Don't know what's wrong with me today. I don't normally sweat this much."

"It's a scorcher, for sure. Are you feeling okay?"

"Yes, just boiling. I guess it's been a long day, and it hasn't helped that my partner's being really flaky."

"Amy, wasn't it?" I recalled how they seemed rather annoyed with each other this morning when they dealt with Neil's unfortunate and untimely demise.

"You've got a great memory. Yes, Amy. She's been off on one today and drove me nuts. At least our shift's over now, which is why I'm here. Needed something to calm me down and fishing always does that."

"What's wrong with your partner? She seemed very nice, and you were both professional. We didn't get the chance to thank you properly earlier, but we appreciated how you helped. It must be a tough job."

"It's very hard, but rewarding too. Thanks for the kind words though. That means a lot. Sometimes we get nothing but grief, so when people acknowledge what we do it makes it worthwhile."

"We really do appreciate it. But what's the issue with your partner? You been a team for long?"

"A few years now. She's great, don't get me wrong, but lately her head's been in the clouds. I don't know what's got into her. She's still the best at her job, and we get along fine, but she keeps disappearing on me. There's always an excuse, like she needs the loo, or she lost track of time when she should know better. It's weird, but she never used to be this way. She was always really dedicated to her work. Now it's like her mind is always on something else."

"Trouble at home maybe? Or money worries?"

"I've asked, but she refuses to admit anything's wrong. She says she isn't with a guy at the moment, so maybe that's it. Although, I think she's got a fella but is keeping it secret. I asked, but she told me to mind my own business. Fair enough, but I always thought we were good mates, not just colleagues, you know?" Peter shrugged, but it clearly rankled that his partner was shutting him out of her life.

"Maybe it's more a problem with work?" I suggested. "It must be a very stressful job. I can't imagine the things you must see."

"It's tough, sure, but so rewarding. Amy's always been great, and she knows so much about everything. More than me. Neither of us are squeamish, which is a deal-breaker in our line of work," he chuckled, "but she's handling things fine like always. I don't know what's got into her. Today's been the worst yet. This morning she vanished just before we were called to the suicide, then again this afternoon. Maybe it's a health issue and she doesn't want to tell me. Yes, that's probably it." Peter brightened, believing he'd figured it out.

"Hopefully it's nothing serious," I noted.

"Um, yeah, course." His smile faded as he said, "She's a great woman, actually, and of course I don't want her to be ill. It's just that an explanation would be good. Sorry, I don't even know why I'm boring you with this. It's not very interesting for you. Just work stuff from a dude you don't even know."

"I really don't mind. It's nice to chat, and if I can help, then I will, but I don't think there's anything I can do. Hopefully, she'll be back to her old self soon enough. Be a good friend and support her. That's all you can do."

"You're right! I will. Now, it's time to fish. How are they biting?"

"Like you wouldn't believe," I grinned. "I got a coolbox full of mackerel. This is the best fishing spot I've ever been to." I explained about being given the details from the man at the fishing shop, but that I'd expected it to be busy.

"So don't tell anyone. I'm amazed Carl at the shop told you about it. He doesn't normally give out such information to strangers."

"Maybe he felt bad for fleecing me. The new reel cost a fortune."

"That's Carl for you," laughed Peter. "I need to stop coming to this place though. For a big guy like me, the climb back up is a killer."

"I think I'm going to struggle," I admitted. "I caught too many and now I have to haul them right back up to the top."

"A fit guy like you can handle it," he grinned, knowing what lay ahead.

As Peter sorted out his gear, I packed my things away then woke Anxious who yawned and stretched then sat in front of Peter, wagging, waiting to be adored. After a fuss, and confirmation he was the cutest dog currently in Wales, Anxious tore off up the steps, barking for me to hurry.

With a grunt, I hefted the weighty coolbox onto my shoulder, said goodbye to Peter, then began the climb. It was arduous, and halfway up I had to rest for a while, but kept the fish on my shoulder as I knew I'd never lift it up again if I lowered it. I heard a cheer from below so assumed Peter was having the same luck I'd had, and it set me to thinking about Amy and wondering why her behaviour had changed. It must be hard to work with someone all day and them to act differently, so my heart went out to him, and her, for whatever the issue was.

The emergency services were so important, and the stress must be awful, so I hoped that she got the problem solved. Both had been so helpful and kind today, even moving Neil so Susie didn't have to see him in such a terrible state, although Peter wasn't too happy about that.

With a deep breath, I continued the climb and almost collapsed when I reached the top where Anxious was sitting with his head cocked, clearly wondering why I was taking so long.

"You try carrying all these fish and see how well you do."

Anxious barked that he wouldn't mind a few right now, but he'd have to wait until later, the same as everyone else, and I had to be mindful of the tiny bones.

Once I'd loaded everything in Vee, I pulled out a chair and sat at the cliff's edge to enjoy the silence, only broken by the gulls screeching and Peter cheering as he hauled in more fish.

The wind cooled my skin, and my energy returned gradually, ready to do battle with the evening of madness I was sure awaited me. One thing Uncle Ernie was good at was throwing a party, and tonight promised to be an epic one on such a special, if very unsettling day.

Chapter 13

As we turned into the car park, I spied the matt black VW ahead. He pulled out of the space, then drove towards me, and I couldn't believe my luck. The driver pulled up alongside me and smiled as he brushed shoulder-length wavy hair from his tanned face.

"We meet again," he laughed.

"And I get my spot back. Did you have a good visit?"

"Mate, this place is the best. The cathedral is awesome, like always, but there's weird stuff going on at the ruin. Hundreds of dogs, and they all got married. I also heard there were some serious incidents. People jumping off the walls. Awful."

"I was here for it all. It's my uncle who got married, along with the dogs."

"Seriously? Mate, that's odd, isn't it?"

"If you knew my family, then not really. Look, great to meet you again, but I'm going to nab the parking space. See you around."

"Yeah, sure thing, and I didn't mean any offence."

"None taken. Don't sweat it." I nodded, then eased past and reversed into the gap just before another car took it.

Anxious was keening to see everyone, but remained close by as we strolled through the grounds, the entire site much more appealing now the tourist rush was over and everything had settled down. We took our time, enjoying the mellow atmosphere, which was just as well as the moment we got to the reception it was bedlam.

I found Mum and Dad with Uncle Ernie at one of the numerous sets of tables and chairs that'd been set up for the buffet, surrounded by a cacophony of chatter and barking. Anxious ran off to find his new best buddy, Special, and I relaxed once he began chasing him and Two-tone around the palace interior with a small group of other dogs. At least they were out of everyone's way.

"What's been going on?" I asked, noting the frowns with concern. "Something else happened? Not another death?"

"No, worse," grumbled Uncle Ernie, putting his head in his hands.

Mum patted his shoulder and said, "Max, there's a problem with the food. Everyone demolished the buffet, so they've eaten, but Freya just heard that the evening caterers for the beach party have had to pull out as their van broke down and they can't make it."

"You aren't using the same people who did the buffet?" I asked.

"It's a different thing entirely. This is all cold cuts and sandwiches. Pork pies and cheese and pickle. The beach party was meant to be a big barbecue with burgers and maybe fish and a relaxed vibe. We've got the booze as it was cheaper to supply it ourselves, but there's no food."

"Then we have a problem we can solve. Just call the local butchers. They should be able to sort you out. Failing that, we'll go to the supermarket. It's not that big a deal is it?"

He brightened, and said, "I suppose not. You're right! Yes, I'll get on it. We've got a few hours until the evening party, to give everyone time to freshen up at their hotels or campsites, but quite a few have already gone to the beach. We need to go and help the staff set things up there soon, but I'm sure we can fix this. Hey, do you think you could go and collect things for us? You can easily fit everything into the campervan."

"Sure. No problem. That's the beauty of my home on wheels. It may be cramped to live in, but it's certainly great for moving things. And actually, I have some very good news. I went for a spot of fishing to clear my head, and I caught absolutely loads of mackerel. If we're careful, there's probably enough for anyone who wants it. It will certainly help."

"So you did go fishing?" said Uncle Ernie. "Good for you. Sorry it's been such a whirlwind of a day. I could do with some downtime myself."

"Then go with Max and get the fish. Give it to Freya and Susie, then pick up the rest of what you need," said Dad. "Me and Jill will help out here, and then we can meet up at the beach later on. You need a break. Freya and Susie do, too, so we'll pitch in and they can go on ahead and set things up without having to rush."

"Now that's an idea I can get behind," beamed Uncle Ernie, his upbeat nature taking over. "But there is one issue." He nodded to me, and Mum and Dad both shook their heads and tutted.

"What's the issue?" I asked.

"Where's your wedding outfit?" he asked, eyeing my clothes with a sad eye.

"I took it off. It's in the campervan. I thought we could change after the wedding?"

"Are we allowed? Freya said I had to stay dressed up."

"You're wearing the exact same clothes you wear every single day," I said, nonplussed. "Fred Perry shirt, braces, trilby hat, dark trousers."

"Yes, but not my best shirt and trousers. And if we're going to the beach I'll get sand everywhere. I'm going to ask if I can change."

"Ask?" scoffed Dad. "The moment you're married you have to ask permission to get changed?" he teased with a smirk.

"It's not like that. I'm being considerate. If Freya wants our outfits to match for the evening party, then I don't mind. But I could do with putting my shorts on."

"Don't you dare," warned Mum. "Nobody wants to see your pasty stick legs."

His optimism faded. "They aren't that bad, are they?"

"The worst," laughed Dad.

"Give me five minutes to tell Freya the good news, then she can make an announcement. We can rustle up everything we need for tonight and finally have fun." Uncle Ernie bounced from his chair, elbows poking out and nearly knocking Dad over.

"We'll be right here," I laughed, pleased his mojo had returned. "But haven't you been having fun? Did you actually enjoy getting married?"

"I'm not sure. I was so stressed about anything going wrong, and worried Freya would change her mind. Plus, having a death on your wedding day isn't the best of omens."

"And now there's two," trilled Mum happily. After getting a good long stare of astonishment from everyone, she conceded, "Not that those poor men deserved such a horrid end, and it's very inconsiderate as this is meant to be a happy day. But off you go, Ernie. We don't want the party to be ruined."

Uncle Ernie hurried off, a spring in his step, so I took a seat and went over what had happened to me since I left. I'd been in two minds about disclosing anything about the threats, but knew I shouldn't hold back such information. For all their wackiness, both often had insights

I'd never have considered. Mostly because they looked at life in a very different way to any other human being I had ever met!

"You should have told us, Son. That's really worrying. What did Min have to say about it?" asked Dad.

"That it was most likely someone from my past being dumb and nothing bad would happen. But they trashed the window of Vee, left a knife, and now these weird things in envelopes. They must be following me everywhere, maybe so close they know where I'm going, as how else could they have been at the campsite?"

"Maybe they overheard someone here talking? We never told anyone, but Ernie might have. Or maybe they did just follow you from the car park. It's damn weird, that's for sure. What are you going to do?"

"He should come home with us. That's what he should do." Mum crossed her arms, her no arguments pose, but this time she wouldn't get her own way.

"I'm not doing that. I can look after myself."

"Not if you're murdered, you can't," she countered expertly.

"Lad's strong and smart. He doesn't want to come home with us. He's got his own life."

"But I don't want my boy to be killed," wailed Mum, jumping up, arms wide, her polka dot dress rustling.

"Nobody's going to kill me. I think it's just someone playing games, but it's a concern, yes. Look, I figured it was best to tell you, but don't worry about me. I'm more concerned about ensuring Uncle Ernie has a fun party and that nobody else dies."

"Especially you," sniffed Mum, making a show of dabbing at her dry eyes.

"Yes, especially me. Here's Uncle Ernie. Not a word."

Dad put a finger to his lips. Mum just turned and blurted, "Max is being threatened by a freaky stalker."

"Mum!"

"He should know. It's important."

"Has something else happened?" asked Uncle Ernie.

"You told him!" asked Mum, aghast.

"I told him earlier," I admitted.

After explaining about the latest incident, we readied to leave, said goodbye to Freya and Susie, then left Mum and Dad with them and returned to the car park.

"Max, there must be at least thirty fish in here," whistled Uncle Ernie when I showed him my haul.

"I know," I grinned. "I got totally carried away, but once they started biting I figured we would use them tonight. Seems like I was right."

"You were." He rubbed his hands together, then asked, "Shall we check out the butchers? See what they've got? And we need bread too. Probably need to do a big shop at Sainsbury's or Tesco."

"Let's do the butchers first before they close. Then we can think about bread and everything else. The main thing is, we have the cakes, we have the guests, and Freya and Susie's team are preparing things at the beach, aren't they?"

"Yep, all that's organised. There's some extra agency staff, we have the DJ setting up there already, with our gear on the way when the lads arrive. Shame my bandmates couldn't come this afternoon, but at least they'll be here for the party."

"That's the spirit. Things are looking up."

It was a short drive to the nearest butchers, and we were in luck. The portly man behind the counter couldn't believe his ears when we explained we wanted a hundred burgers, and he eagerly set about making them as he had hardly any already made. While he did that, we hit the supermarket, stocked up on everything else we needed, then returned to the butchers and loaded the meat into Vee. Anxious was beside himself, eyes bugging, as pack after pack of burgers and sausages were stowed in the coolboxes we'd had to buy to keep everything fresh.

After explaining to the starving sausage muncher that he'd have to wait a while yet, he decided the best thing he could do was to keep guard, so sat between the coolboxes in the back and kept an eye on things just in case there were any sausage thieves—apart from him—on the loose.

With us both feeling positive about things, we jumped back in and I started up the van, but then I asked, "How is everyone getting to the beach? It's a bit of a trek, isn't it?"

"Not too far, and everything's been arranged. Most of the guests are staying at the same hotel as it's one that caters for dogs too. We got a massive discount as there were so many of them, and even got the hotel to lay on transport. The ones who are camping will use their own vehicles. Some at the hotel will, too, but I think they enjoy the communal atmosphere of everyone in a coach together. Nothing stranger than folk, right?"

"You got that right. It must be chaos in a coach full of excited dogs and even more excited owners. Especially on a day like today with the weddings. Did everyone get married in the end?"

"They did. Amazingly, it went rather well. Freya and Susie were pleased. I can't believe Susie's handling this so well. Her husband is actually dead. How she can smile and continue with the day is incredible."

"It clearly hasn't upset her that much. Most people would never cope like she has. You don't think she could have something to do with it, do you? It would explain why she's acting this way."

"Nephew, she wouldn't hurt a fly. But think about it. What else could she do? She didn't want to let Freya and me down, or the others. She's a trooper, that's what she is. Now, let's get this stuff over to the beach. We can get it in the shade, pack more ice in, and hopefully we can leave the staff to run things then."

"I'm happy to pitch in and cook if you want. Nothing fancy, just barbecue the fish and burgers." Anxious barked from the rear, causing us both to chuckle, so I turned and confirmed, "Yes, and the sausages." Satisfied, he turned his attention back to the coolboxes.

Buoyed by our luck, and with stomachs beginning to rumble, I made the slow, and presumably convoluted drive to Whitesands Bay. Six minutes later we arrived. Pulling to a stop, we gawped at each other then burst out laughing. When we'd recovered, I said, "Sorry, I know I said it would be a rough drive with tiny roads and endless traffic lights for non-existent roadworks, but, um, that was easy."

"Guess it really is a small place. We got here quicker than I could eat a sausage." Anxious barked, so Uncle Ernie laughed and corrected, "But yes, Anxious could devour quite a few in that time."

"Let's get things sorted." I nodded to my happy uncle then we let the steely-eyed guard dog out. He kept watch over proceedings while we unloaded, before skipping off to sniff the various vehicles in case any starving thieves were lurking with knife and fork at the ready.

The car park was rammed with vehicles. Cars, campers, motorhomes, and the coach for the wedding party, so we carried what we could down towards the beach, the sound of people and animals deafening the closer we got.

We exchanged a concerned look, as what on earth had happened now, so we sped up, Anxious barking in a very worrying tone.

"What's going on?" I asked Freya and Susie who were retreating up the path at a fast clip, the guests and staff bunched together with the dogs mostly on leads.

Flustered, and both looking ready to burst into tears, Freya spluttered, "No dogs allowed."

"Allowed where?" asked Uncle Ernie, as confused as me.

"On the beach. We can't have the party here."

"What do you mean?" asked Uncle Ernie, still not understanding. "You got special permission, didn't you? You arranged it. I know you can't exactly book a beach, but you were told you could have the party here."

"It's my fault," stammered Susie, snatching a glance at her sister.

"No, it isn't. Just one of those things."

"I'm to blame!" shouted Susie, a vein throbbing under her right eye, her cheeks burning. "I made the arrangements with the right people, got permission for the weddings at the ruin, and was told we could have the party on the beach, but I think I forgot to mention there would be dogs for the evening too. Now there's some bloke there saying we can't go on the beach. I promised to clear up, but he was adamant. Said it's too busy, even now, and dogs are only allowed strictly between September and May. No animals at all now. What are we going to do?" she wailed, bending over and physically urging, beyond distraught.

"Problem?" asked a familiar voice.

I turned and found myself face to face with the other campervan owner from the car park. "Oh, hi. Yes, a bit of a problem. We were meant to be having a wedding party here this evening, but there's been a mix up and we aren't allowed dogs on the beach. And this is as much about them as us."

"Ah, the bunch of crazies from earlier," he said, grinning at everyone and flicking a lock off his face, causing Susie to gasp and Freya to sigh. Admittedly, he was a good-looking man, but it was still an extreme reaction.

"We aren't crazy," said Susie, recovering her composure somewhat. "But this day's turning into a disaster."

"Never fear, Dubman is here," he grinned.

"Dubman?" asked Uncle Ernie.

"Yeah, I'm a Vdub guy like this dude here. Got the nickname after a while on the road, and it stuck. You can call me Roger if you want, but, you know, Dubman is way cooler."

"Much," agreed Uncle Ernie, taking to Dubman like I had, and the two ladies clearly had too.

"Anyway, let me sort this. I know a guy." Dubman winked, then wandered off with his phone to his ear.

"What's he going to do?" whispered Uncle Ernie.

"No idea. Why are you whispering?"

"I'm not sure," he said quietly, glancing towards Dubman. "Who is that guy?"

"I just met him in the car park earlier. He's a vanlifer. Has a very cool matt black eighties campervan. We swapped spots."

"How'd you mean? Swapped spots? Like acne? That's super weird, Max."

"Car park spots. I was leaving, he was pulling in. Then when I pulled in, he was leaving. Perfect timing."

"And was it love at first sight?" he teased. "He's a handsome bloke. Nearly as good-looking as you."

"You think?" I found myself toying with my hair, and grinning stupidly, so tried to control myself.

"Yes, you're a catch, Max," laughed Uncle Ernie. "Quick, act normal. Here he comes."

Uncle Ernie, Freya, Susie, and now Mum and Dad stood to attention like they were waiting for their names to be called as Dubman walked leisurely back to us. "The Dubman has saved the day," he announced loudly.

And it turned out, he really had.

Chapter 14

Ten minutes later, the wedding party was happily exiting the coach, cars, and vans after following Dubman along a sandy track that petered out in a large, almost deserted car park.

Everyone gathered around as he explained in his own relaxed way that he knew someone on the local council and there was no problem with us using this smaller, but still beautiful stretch of beach for the party. Dogs were allowed here all year, so there was no issue with that, and although there wasn't exactly a formal permit as it was after hours, Dubman assured us that we wouldn't be bothered and could party to our hearts' content.

"Thank you so much," gushed Freya as she, Susie, and Rachel crowded him. I wouldn't say they were drooling, but I wouldn't say they were sad either.

"Hey, for my new friends, no problem." Dubman winked at me, then excused himself and came over to where I waited with Uncle Ernie and my folks.

"We really appreciate this," I said. "How do you know a guy on the council?"

"I get about over the years and it's always good to have friends in high places."

"It is," agreed Mum, applying lipstick and getting a filthy look from Dad, which she chose to ignore.

Dubman pulled me to one side, and once we were away from the increasingly rowdy group, he told me, "Actually, I just made that up. I didn't speak to anyone. How would I know a bloke on the council?"

"What!? We can't have a party here then. We'll get into trouble."

"Mate, you gotta relax. Who's going to tell? You guys set up your stuff, have a fun time, and chill. This isn't a popular beach as it's not good for surfing, and besides, I guarantee you won't be disturbed."

"How can you guarantee that?"

"Because I might not know anyone on the council, but I do know the owner of the property over there." He pointed to a large building several fields away. "This section of beach is his. It's private land, so you can do what you want."

"You're making that up, too, aren't you? You can't own the beach in this country, can you?"

Dubman laughed as he slapped me on the back and admitted, "Not exactly. Okay, the truth is I didn't want everyone to be disappointed, or for your party to be ruined, so I figured this would help you out."

"What's this?" asked Freya as she and Susie came to check on us.

"We don't have permission to use the beach. Dubman was just pretending."

"Oh no! Really?" Freya was distraught, and glanced back to the waiting group.

"Max, I was teasing," chuckled Dubman. "You should have seen your face. Of course I know a guy. He said it's fine. I'm a bit of a joker, but I'm sorry. Everyone chill. Look, here's the bloke from the other beach now."

As the man emerged from his car, Dubman took Freya and Susie over to speak to him. He drove off a few minutes later.

I joined them and they explained that he patrolled the beaches to ensure everyone was obeying the rules, but there was nothing about large groups gathering on the beach. Dogs were allowed, so as long as we didn't run amok or make a mess we were free to do what we wanted now it was the evening.

Freya and Susie thanked Dubman, invited him to the party, then left to arrange everything and get set up.

"You should stay. We wouldn't be doing any of this without you," I told him.

"Nah, mate, I got things to do. Which means, beers to drink back at my pitch. Another time?"

"Of course. I'm staying for a few days, so maybe we'll bump into each other."

"It's a small place, so yeah, see you around, Max." Dubman said his goodbyes to everyone then left, kicking up sand as he raced away.

"He was nice," said Mum, fanning herself with her hand.

"You fancied him," accused Dad with a pout.

"Don't be silly. He wasn't my type. Too much of a hippy like our Max. All that luscious long hair and those dark, brooding brown eyes. Not my thing at all."

Mum wandered off to help with things while Dad grumbled then turned to me and asked, "Think she'll ever leave me?"

I thought he was joking, but then I understood that no matter how happy a couple are, maybe there's always that nagging that one day, just possibly, things might go wrong. Even Dad was scared the love of his life might leave.

"Dad, she loves you more than ever. Of course she won't leave you."

"I hope not. I love that woman so much. She might be crazy, but I adore her."

"I know you do. And she feels the same way. Trust me, you have nothing to worry about."

"Even from hunky young men with lovely hair?"

"Yes, even from them. She wants you, and that will always be enough for Mum."

Dad beamed as he puffed out his chest and sighed. "You're a good son. Come on, Max, let's make this a party to remember."

More vehicles arrived, having been given the new directions by Susie and Freya, so with almost everyone now here, we helped the team to take everything onto the beach and began setting things up. The DJ got things going within minutes with laid-back tunes, getting everyone into a mellow party mood after the upset and turmoil.

It was a simple setup with a small sound system and decent speakers, but nothing that would blow your eardrums. Just enough to entertain. With their team busy, we got the tables for food and drinks laid out quickly, then hauled the coolboxes and various items onto the beach and got several large barbecues lit. They needed at least forty minutes for the charcoal to reach the right temperature, which gave us plenty of time to sort everything out properly while the steady thud of dub reggae lifted the atmosphere and calmed everyone's nerves.

With the waves lapping at the shore, the guests laughing and drinking, the dogs racing around happily, and everyone mindful of ensuring not a single piece of litter was dropped and the dogs were cleaned up after immediately, it couldn't have been a nicer evening.

The temperature was perfect here, with a gentle breeze coming in from the sea, and I finally allowed myself to relax and wander down to the shore now everything was ready for dinner later.

With mellow beats the backdrop to this perfect summer's evening, I could have been anywhere in the world. I pictured myself on a tropical island, Barbados maybe, with palm trees swaying, a hammock waiting for me, possibly a cocktail with a garish umbrella, ice tinkling against the frosty rim, and a deep serenity took me over.

Anxious took a break from the dog melee to join me, and splashed about happily, stomping down fast, eyes glued to the water as he focused on trying to catch the tiny fish that darted between my feet as I wriggled my toes in the sand.

As noise levels rose, I turned to see that Ernie's bandmates had finally arrived, lugging guitars and even several drums. I waved, but remained rooted to the spot, the smiling faces and the happy animals giving me a deep sense of gratitude for the chance to be part of what had to be the craziest day I'd ever experienced.

In my relaxed state, I had if not an epiphany of sorts, but a familiar feeling of answers forming just out of reach. I didn't know how, but things were slowly coming together, and I realised I was coming close to getting an answer. I also realised that I'd completely overlooked one important thing, and called for Anxious then hurried over to Uncle Ernie, said hello to the other members of The Skankin' Skeletons, then explained what I had to do. He offered to come with me, but I said there was no need, so after telling my folks what I was up to, and them insisting on tagging along, we bundled into Vee and returned with all haste to the Bishop's Palace.

"Why are we going back there again?" asked Dad from beside me.

"To search for clues, you utter numpty," hollered Mum from the back where she was sitting with Anxious curled up in her lap.

"Don't you numpty me," warned Dad, turning to try to stare down Mum, and failing, obviously. "I'll get an inferiority complex and lose my self-confidence. You shouldn't call me names."

"You call me names all the time," countered Mum. "Pilchard, daft old bint, wally, plonker. You even called me a silly moo once," she added, her tone dangerously low.

"That… that was in the heat of the moment, and I never did it again," he said hurriedly. "Tell her, Max," he pleaded.

"Keep me out of this," I laughed. "But he's right, Mum. You shouldn't call him names. He's such a fragile man, with hardly any confidence, and you might push him over the edge and he'll never go outside the house again."

We burst out laughing, as we knew the one thing neither of them lacked was confidence. They might have missed the handing out of bleedin' obvious, but got a triple helping of unwarranted confidence instead.

With my excitable parents belting out *A Little Less Conversation*, we thankfully arrived back at the car park in under ten minutes, and they killed the song as I killed the engine. After my ears stopped ringing, and Anxious finally gave up on the howling, we got out and wandered over to the Bishop's Palace. It was so different without the crowds and only a few tourists out for an evening stroll or sitting enjoying fish and chips on the grass.

We made our way into the now gloomy interior, and I shivered.

"Everything seems bigger now it's empty. The walls look higher and much more dangerous," noted Dad.

"Those silly men," tutted Mum. "It's such a shame what happened to them. Nobody deserves to go out like that."

"That's very kind, Mum."

"I do have feelings! I know sometimes I'm rather oblivious and make light of even the most terrible things, but it's my way of coping. The poor men."

I gave her a cuddle and said, "It's okay. We'll get justice for them," then stepped back.

"Course we will," she squealed. "Now, let's go find some clues and blow this case wide open. Ooh, I can't wait to see the look on that stupid detective's face when he finds out we solved this. He'll be so annoyed." Mum rubbed her hands together, beaming at the prospect, her empathy gone.

After making a circuit of the empty space, we managed to find the way up to the parapet, but it wasn't as easy as on the east side. At the top, there was no nice safe space to move around, just a ledge and a very long drop. How Mum managed in her high heels was a mystery, and how she wasn't chafing from sand was testament to her dedication to unsuitable footwear.

"What are we looking for?" asked Mum, frowning as she peered over the edge.

"Don't get too close, love," gasped Dad, hurrying over.

"I'm fine. As sure-footed as a goat."

"With legs to match," said Dad, regretting it instantly as he got walloped. But Mum overexerted herself, and as Dad moved back so only received a glancing blow, her slap kept on going and she spun, cried out, and her arms flailed.

Dad grabbed her forearm and yanked Mum away from certain death, and they both fell backwards onto the uneven ledge in a heap, gasping for breath out of fear. Mum rolled off him and sat bolt upright, utterly composed until she noted the dust on her dress. She brushed it off casually, turned to Dad, and said, "Wowee! That was close."

Dad remained prone, eyes shut, face locked in terror.

"Mum, are you okay? Are you in shock? Dad saved you. You nearly died."

"I'm fine, but my dress is dirty. I'll have to change."

"You will not," mumbled Dad as he scrambled to his feet and reached out then hauled Mum up. "You look beautiful."

They stared into each other's eyes for a moment, then kissed, and kept on kissing. I had to turn away, as it's one thing seeing your folks give each other a quick peck, quite another to see them snog each other's faces off.

I coughed politely, my back to them, and only once Mum giggled and Dad cleared his throat did I dare turn back around.

"Er, sorry about that," said Dad, adjusting his sleeves then running a comb through disheveled hair.

"Yes, sorry, love. Don't know what came over us."

"The relief that you didn't both die, I'm guessing. But next time, please save the smooching for when I'm not around."

"You can count on it!" Dad slapped Mum's bum and she giggled.

I shook my head and sighed, but something caught my attention from the corner of my eye and I bent, then got onto my hands and knees. I crawled forward to the edge of the wall and stared down at what was undoubtedly another clue.

"A wedding ring?" I asked myself. I almost reached out and picked it up, but instead took a photo first before carefully prising it from where it had lodged between two loose stones.

"Another ring?" asked Dad as he and Mum took several steps closer then stopped, mindful of the drop.

"It is. Not an engagement ring, though. Just a simple gold band. Most likely a wedding ring. What would it be doing up here? Do you think Marcus dropped it?"

"What would he be doing with it?" asked Dad. "They didn't exchange rings for the dogs, did they? Wouldn't surprise me if they did. Bunch of crazies if you ask me."

"Don't judge them," scolded Mum. "It's sweet they want their pets to be married. And besides, it's just innocent fun. But no, they didn't use rings."

"Mum's right. And even if they did, why would he drop it like this unless he was holding it before he jumped? Maybe he was meant to be getting married soon? Maybe the wedding fell through, or maybe…"

"What?" they both asked, leaning forward, faces eager.

"Maybe the killer dropped it."

"A ring for each man?" frowned Mum. "One engagement ring, and one wedding ring? That's dumb. I bet it's like the other one and they got dropped years ago by people climbing the walls or proposals that went wrong, and because they're so small, they never got found when the place gets cleaned. That makes more sense."

"You're right, it does, and maybe that's all it is. But it's still a coincidence. Let's keep looking, then I suppose I better report this to the police."

We carefully, meaning the two adult terrors stayed well away from the edge and hardly moved, searched around the ledge and wall. I found a ring pull from a soft drink can, an empty packet of Walker's cheese and onion crisps, a sandwich container, two empty cans of Heineken, and a wrapper from a Fudge bar.

"Dammit!" I cursed, not like me at all.

"What is it?" asked Dad.

"A Fudge wrapper!" I studied the offending article, butterflies in my belly.

"Argh! No, I won't have it," he insisted.

"Not a Fudge?" squealed Mum, wrapping her arms around Dad and putting her face to his chest.

"I'm afraid so. And we know what this means, don't we?" I said, convinced they did. "How long has it been?"

"About ten years, and I thought we'd finally escaped the curse of the finger of Fudge," said Dad once Mum plucked up enough courage to turn and face me.

"Me too. It's so hard to avoid, but I haven't so much as looked at the chocolate bar counter in a shop or garage the whole time."

"Neither have we," said Dad, patting Mum's head as if that was reassuring.

"What will we do?" wailed Mum. "I can't go through life like this. It's so unfair. The evil advert makers should be shot. Fancy doing that to poor people just wanting to get on with their lives."

"Utterly criminal," agreed Dad.

"They must have used maniacs to write the jingle," I agreed, shuddering, but unable to discard the wrapper now I'd picked it up, and unable to look away from the seemingly innocuous tiny sleeve of plastic.

"Drop it, Son, and maybe it won't happen," suggested Dad with a wince.

"I can't be a litter lout, but now I'm stuck. Look at it. It's so cute and bright, and oh boy, do you remember the taste? They don't last long, but while they do it's heaven."

"Stop it! Just stop it," wailed Mum. "Don't do this to us, Max. Please," she pleaded. "Not again."

"I'm sorry, but it's too late."

We nodded to each other, and with a gleam in our eyes we hurried from the edge, retrieved Anxious, then raced to the nearest shop and bought three Fudges.

Life would never be the same again.

Chapter 15

"So nice." Mum sighed as she nibbled gently at the already half-eaten finger of Fudge.

"The best," agreed Dad, eyeing the remains of his tiny chocolate bar with a worried frown.

"Don't even think it," I warned, lamenting that I had only a mouthful of my own treat left.

Anxious whined at our feet, staring up dolefully as we huddled close on the bench outside the shop like three junkies unable to wait any longer for our fix.

"Sorry, buddy, but you're out of luck this time. Chocolate is bad for dogs, and even if it wasn't you wouldn't be getting any." I handed him a biscuit instead and he settled happily, but I knew what he was thinking. "Me want Cadbury's Fudge."

"We caved!" grumbled Dad as he popped the last morsel into his mouth then scrunched up the wrapper and dropped it into the bin.

"It's your fault," I accused. "I would have resisted if it wasn't for you two."

"Liar," said Mum, nibbling a little more. Dad shifted closer to her, but she slapped his hand as he reached out with shaking fingers.

"I would have. I have willpower." Regrettably, the time had come, so I finished it off, disposed of my wrapper, too, and we sat in silence watching with our mouths watering as Mum relished hers in excruciatingly tiny bites.

"How can you do that?" asked Dad. "It's not possible to eat one that slowly."

"I can control myself. And besides, it's fun to watch you dolts squirm." She giggled, then tore the rest from the wrapper and popped it between ruby-red lips.

Dad and I gasped, desperate to taste what she was tasting.

"Is it lovely?" I asked, licking my lips and leaning in close to smell her chocolate breath.

"Breathe this way," insisted Dad, eyes glazing over.

"You both stop that!" warned Mum as she closed her eyes and groaned with delight as she swallowed.

And then it began.

It started with Dad humming happily to himself, then I found my foot tapping, and then Mum began drumming a tune on the bench. Before we were even aware of it, we were singing the jingle to the finger of Fudge advert that had been both the delight and scourge of my youth.

The advert was around in my parents' time but had made a comeback for a short while when I was a kid, and although I had only ever seen it a few times it simply didn't matter. Mum and Dad had both battled with their obsession through their impressionable years, and then into teenagerhood, and when they met each other both still had a terrible addiction. Together, they'd managed to beat it, but when the adverts suddenly began to appear when I was young, and I saw them in the shops, they'd caved and let me have one.

It started simply. I had a single treat and they managed to resist. But the next time they decided they'd have one, too, and soon it became a daily ritual to race eagerly to the corner shop and get ourselves one of the tiny little beauties in a bright wrapper.

It had taken over ten years for us to break free of this terrible affliction, and now we were right back where we started. It was the song. That was the issue. Yes, the bar itself tasted divine, and yes, it was small, and yes, only a hundred calories, but what sealed the deal was the combination of wrapper, what was inside, the jingle, and the obscenely smart advert itself.

A young lad happily eating his treat, his mum smiling away as the song played out.

"It's full of Cadbury goodness, but very small and neat. A finger of Fudge is just enough to give your kids a treat," sang Dad merrily as he surreptitiously got to his feet and began walking backwards towards the shop like we couldn't see.

"No, don't do it!" I warned, lunging for him.

"I have to. Forgive me, both of you, but if I'm not back soon don't come looking for me. No, don't stare! I know I'm disgusting. I'm not worthy of your love. Look away. Look away!" he screeched and raced for the door.

Mum vaulted the bench, I jumped right, and we grabbed an arm each as the shop bell rang. We pulled Dad out, kicking and screaming about it being only a few calories and he promised to still eat his dinner, but we ignored him and pressed him onto the bench, keeping a firm hold on the shaking mess of a man.

"Let me go!" he wailed, but we held him fast until the sugar rush faded and he was left looking nothing but ashamed. Dad hung his head and whispered, "Don't look at me. I know I did wrong. But it's the song. I can't stop it playing in my head."

"We know," soothed Mum. "It's the same for us, love. It's a terrible thing they did to us, those fiends, but together we can be strong. We failed this time, but no more. No more, dammit!" she roared, fist clenched and shaking it at the sky. "We won't be swayed again. Never!"

"Not even one teensy, tiny one?" I asked, glancing at the shop, my bum already lifting from the bench and my mouth watering.

"Max, not you too?" wailed Dad as he grabbed me, our roles reversing.

Steeling myself, I sat, determined not to be so weak.

"It's full of Cadbury goodness," I sang, almost in a dream state, and I knew for certain that for the next few days it would go around and around like an earworm and I'd find it hard to focus unless I concentrated really hard.

"We're good people," said Dad. "We don't deserve this. How could we cave so quickly?"

"It was the wrapper, wasn't it?" said Mum.

"Oh no, that reminds me! I have to phone the detective about the wedding ring. We totally forgot."

"Yes, do that," insisted Mum. "It'll take our minds off things."

With shaking hands, I pulled out my phone and made the call. DI Davies wasn't happy to hear from me, but when I explained why I was calling he perked up and promised to send someone over to pick up the ring within minutes.

True to his word, and with us trying to control our jitters, a policeman arrived on foot and I handed over the latest find.

Alone once more, I suggested we return to the party, which by now should be in full swing and the barbecues would be primed for cooking. Thinking about the mackerel and burgers allowed me to put the chocolate addiction out of my mind for a moment, but it was still there, lurking, waiting to pounce when I least suspected it. I prayed this time I'd be able to break the cycle before I became a gibbering wreck and a corner shop addict. Would I end my days lurking in the shadows beside the door, asking for change so I could rush inside, slam my coins down on the counter with chocolate-covered hands, and snatch another bar of sweet delight? I shuddered at the thought.

"The rings are perplexing," mused Dad. "On the one hand, it might be important, but on the other, it could mean nothing."

"Well, that was absolutely not helpful," snapped Mum. "We know that already."

"I was just thinking out loud to get it straight in my head. Could either man have been about to propose or get married?"

"Neil was already married," I reminded him. "And Marcus was there because his dog was getting married, not him. And none of the dogs were being given rings. How would they wear them?"

"Maybe he'd got one to give to the dog his dog was marrying? Or maybe to give to his own," mused Dad. "He might have just wanted to have something to remember the day by."

"It's possible," I conceded. "But what are the odds of both men dropping the rings? That's not very likely."

"But not impossible."

"True. The most likely scenario is what you said earlier, Dad, and that they got lost over the years and never found as they rolled into a gap in the walls. Might have been there for decades."

"Or," said Mum brightly, "someone put them there on purpose."

We both turned to her, intrigued, and I encouraged, "Go on."

"Um, that was it. But it was a good idea, right?"

"It was, Mum. But why would someone plant the rings? And if they did, why make it so hard to find them? The police didn't discover the gold one, we did, so it might never have been found."

"But it was, wasn't it? Maybe the killer assumed the police would find both easily."

"You might be right. But it still doesn't explain why. It's certainly worth considering though." As I mulled it over, I spied Amy the paramedic on the other side of the road. It took me a moment to identify her, as I'd only ever seen her in her green uniform and lugging medical equipment, but it was definitely her.

"Cooee!" Mum waved as she called to Amy, who either didn't hear or chose not to acknowledge us, so continued on her way.

"I don't think she knew you were calling to her," said Dad.

"That was so rude!" pouted Mum. "Of course she heard. Who else would I be waving to?"

"Mum, it could have been to anyone. She didn't even look our way. Let's go. We need to get to the party."

We followed after Amy who was heading towards the car park, taking her time, clearly pre-occupied. We almost caught up with her, but then she turned off the street into a newsagents and we passed by. Dad's footsteps faltered and then he stopped, and I turned just in time to see him ready to bolt.

"Stay strong," I encouraged, grabbing his arm.

"I just want to have a teeny taste. A tiny bite. I won't take long," he whined.

"No way. Admit you're an addict and resist. We are. Right, Mum?"

Mum breezed past us, eyes glazed as she headed for the shop. "Eh? What's that? Gosh, was I about to go inside? Stop me! I can't help myself."

Dad's own cravings forgotten, he took one side while I took the other, and together we pulled Mum away. At that moment, the door opened and the annoying buzzer many shops had rang out loud as Amy emerged with a pack of crisps and stuffing a few other snacks into her jacket pocket. Even though the day was warm, she wore faded jeans, hiking boots, a simple red shirt, and a Wrangler black denim jacket.

"Oh, hello," she said with a cautious smile, clearly wondering why we had hold of Mum.

"Hello, love. Getting some treats, are you?" asked Mum merrily.

"Er, yes. I'm a bit of a crisp addict," she admitted.

"Nothing to be ashamed of. We all have our own snack addictions. Lovely evening, isn't it?"

"Yes, very. Shouldn't you be at your party? Did it get cancelled because of earlier?"

"We just came from the beach. Now we're going back. We've been having another look at where Marcus fell from to see if we could find anything."

"And did you?" she leaned closer, keen to hear, but Anxious growled and she backed away. "Gosh, are you alright, Anxious?"

Anxious barked, but remained sitting between us.

"What are you doing?" I asked. "This is the woman who helped when the men died," I told him. Facing Amy, I explained, "Sorry, but he gets like this sometimes when he's tired. And he's probably hungry."

A bark in the affirmative confirmed my suspicions.

"No problem. So, did you find anything? Are you still convinced it was foul play?"

"We didn't find anything, no. And it's seeming more and more likely that the deaths weren't murder."

"That's good news, isn't it?"

"I suppose. But that's enough about that. You're welcome to join us at the party if you'd like? I don't know if you have plans, but if you want to come, you are officially invited. There will be food and drinks and music. It'll be fun."

"That's very kind of you, but, er, I'm not sure."

"Come on, love, it'll be great. Unless you had plans?" asked Mum.

"It's Saturday night and I just came out of the newsagents with a bag of crisps and a pocketful of chocolate. So, no, I don't have plans," she chuckled, casting a nervous glance up the street.

"Then it's settled," said Dad. "You can come with us in the van."

"I don't want to impose. No, I shouldn't crash your party. I'm not even sure it's right. I dealt with the problems earlier today, so the last person anyone wants to see is me."

"Everyone thought you did a wonderful job," I told her. "You were very kind to Susie, moving Neil so she didn't have to see him like that."

"And I got into trouble for it. Maybe I'll stay here and eat my crisps. I can't get enough of the salt and vinegar ones."

"Nonsense!" said Mum in a tone that demanded obedience. "It's our way of saying thank you.

"Then okay! Why not?" Amy smiled and allowed Mum and Dad to lace their arms through hers, then we returned to the van, Amy gripped tightly as my folks ensured she couldn't change her mind.

Anxious rode up front with me and Dad while Mum and Amy sat together in the back. Whenever I glanced in the mirror, Amy was studying the campervan interior, most likely as she felt rather uncomfortable beside a woman with bright red hair grinning at her the whole time.

Luckily for our prisoner it was a short drive, and in under ten minutes we were out of the van and making our way back to the beach. Mum and Dad went on ahead while I walked beside Amy with Anxious trotting in front but staying close.

"Sorry to drag you off like this," I said. "If you really don't want to be here I can take you back. Mum and Dad can be rather overbearing and don't always listen."

"They're sweet, if rather pushy," she agreed.

"I know. They don't always pick up on even very obvious hints. You want to go home?"

"Max, I wouldn't put you to all that trouble."

"It's no trouble. I assume you live in the area?"

"Just outside town. I like wandering around in the evening when it's quiet. Tourism is great for the city, but it doesn't make it feel like home, if that makes sense."

"Perfect sense. You want to see familiar faces, not a bunch of tourists who you'll never see again. I get it. I assume most of your work is dealing with visitors, not the locals?"

"It's usually sunstroke or people hurting themselves when they go hiking. We get loads of twisted ankles and broken legs from falls. The winter is quiet, but summer is usually crazy busy."

"I can imagine. Were you born here?"

"Born here, grew up here, went to the nearest university, and never really left." Amy glanced at me then away, her voice flat.

"It doesn't sound like you're too happy about that. You never wanted to leave?"

"Max, sometimes you just look back on your life and realise that it wasn't what you thought it would be. Does that make sense?"

"Of course."

"I never had a plan beyond becoming a paramedic. Even that wasn't a plan so much as just an idea for a steady job. I thought I'd go and work in a big city, Manchester or Liverpool, maybe even London, but I never got around to it. I started work as soon as I was qualified, began earning decent money, and just stayed. I love it here, and it is home, but I should have been more adventurous."

"Nothing wrong with staying where you grew up. It's a beautiful part of the world. No husband or children?"

"No children, and the husband thing is complicated." Amy's tone made it obvious the subject was closed.

"Sorry to pry. I wasn't being nosy. Well, maybe a little," I teased to lighten the mood.

Amy laughed then told me, "I'd rather not talk about it. What about you? Are you really living in your van? I was studying it on the trip, and it's so well laid out. I bet it's great fun."

"It sure is. It's the best thing I ever did for my mental health. I'm finally the man I always wanted to be. A fresh start."

"Maybe that's what I need," she sighed, rubbing at her cheek rather too hard. "Something to snap me out of things. Do something wild and different."

"It's never too late. But vanlife isn't for everyone. It's cramped, there's no washing machine, shower, or toilet, and I haven't gone through a winter yet."

"But it's an adventure, isn't it? You're doing things, seeing things. Meeting all kinds of people."

"I have met some incredible people. And there have certainly been plenty of adventures. I keep getting embroiled in one mystery after another." I stopped, and Amy turned back. "Can I ask you a question?"

"Sure, but I might not be able to answer you. If it's about the deaths, then there's only so much I can discuss."

"I understand. What do you think happened?"

Amy frowned. "They fell."

"Yes, but by their own volition?"

"I heard you all talking about there being no way the men would jump, but I've seen this kind of thing before. Max, nobody knows what goes on in another person's head. You might think they're fine, but they aren't."

"So they jumped?" I pushed.

"I honestly have no idea. I'm not a detective. All I know is they were both dead. That's what I do. I try to save people, but sometimes it's too late. Today it was too late for them both."

"But two jumpers in one day?"

"It's very odd, granted, but the other explanation isn't exactly likely either. Maybe the first death gave the other man the idea. There was a lot of upset, I heard, so maybe he just copied what happened." Amy shrugged.

"Sorry to spoil the mood. How about we enjoy the party? I'm going to help with the cooking, but feel free to do whatever you want."

Another minute and we were in the thick of it. I lost sight of Amy as Uncle Ernie hurried over and ushered me to the barbecue.

Chapter 16

With the sound system blaring, people laughing and chatting, dogs playing, and smoke filling the air, I was in my element. With Crocs off, sand between my toes, and tongs in hand, I set to work cooking burgers on one barbecue, sausages on another, and the numerous mackerel that Uncle Ernie had cleaned expertly on yet another.

Freya, Susie, and Rachel worked with the rest of the team to serve everyone as they queued for their food, helping themselves to various salads and leftovers from the buffet lunch served earlier but kept cool and fresh.

Mum and Dad pitched in, too, chatting happily to everyone as they squirted ketchup or mayonnaise onto burgers, or slapped slices of cheese onto buns. Everyone smiled, was friendly, and eager to eat, and all the while my best buddy remained by my side, eyes on the sausages, daring me to burn or drop one so he could snaffle it.

Having only cooked small portions for months, apart from a single stint in a pub kitchen, I wasn't sure if I would absolutely hate this return to cooking for the masses, but I surprised myself with how much I enjoyed it. Whereas before it was fine-dining with an obsessive eye on every minute detail, this was a different world entirely. One made up of repetition and a relaxed approach to the timing.

I soon got into a rhythm of flipping burgers, turning sausages, and checking on the fish until I had it down to an art. All the old skills came back, and I got into a familiar zone where I was almost at one with the food and could tell when everything was cooked to perfection. More than just sight, it was the sound, smell, and sizzle combining and noted in an instant that allowed me to know with an almost sixth sense when everything was ready.

With us working well as a team, we had the perfect production line set up and within half an hour everyone had a plate of food and many were back for seconds.

Times like this made me realise how much I enjoyed the art of cooking, but I had no desire to ever return to the stress of 3-star restaurant pressure where presentation often overtook the most important thing when it came to food. The taste.

I was relaxed, took a few burned sausages when I became distracted in my stride, and went with the flow. The good mood permeating our party meant the little guy and a few of his buddies got to eat more than was sensible, but not enough to hinder their desire to run around enjoying themselves once I told them they'd had all they would get.

With the last few burgers sizzling away nicely, and the fish still in plentiful supply, and a handful of sausages moved to the edge of the grill for anyone who wanted them, everyone had settled into groups or were enjoying strolling along the beach on a perfect summer's evening.

"Time for us to eat?" I asked the others.

Everyone agreed it was, so Freya and Rachel set up the plates and buns and I dropped a burger onto each then Mum and Dad sorted out sauces and salads while I dealt with the fish. The skin was crispy, the inside steaming, so I plated them and we settled on the sand and tucked in.

"Wow, this mackerel is so good," said Uncle Ernie, licking his lips then pulling a piece of fish off the bone.

My mouth was filled with a taste unlike any other, and I grinned. "Nothing beats fresh fish," I sighed. "It's completely different to even day old fish. You can practically taste the sea."

"You did a great job, Max. Thank you," beamed Freya, looking more relaxed than she had all day.

"Thank you. I'm glad I could help out. You've had such a busy day. You deserve to take it easy now. Is there anything else that needs doing?"

"No, nothing. We'll let the staff clean everything away and we're going to enjoy the rest of the evening. Ernie, you and the guys are still playing, aren't you?"

"If they manage to stand," laughed Uncle Ernie, nodding at his bandmates sitting over by the DJ with empty plates beside them and drinks in hand.

"This has been a strange day," said Rachel, hugging Freya. "You both dealt with it so well. I'm so sorry about what happened, Susie, but you've been so brave."

Susie smiled, genuine and warm, and said, "I've been trying to just get on with things. Tomorrow is when this will all seem real, but right now it's like a dream. I don't want to think about any of it. I just want this day to be over and for my sister to be happy."

Freya pulled both in tight and the three women embraced. When they broke apart, they jumped to their feet and organised the staff who were already on the ball and clearing away the food and collecting plates, ensuring there was no mess.

"How come the paramedic came back with you?" asked Uncle Ernie, nodding in her direction.

She was laughing as she chatted with Patrick, the man whose dog was to marry Marcus', and I noted that the chihuahua was clutched tight in his arms, fast asleep. I hadn't even thought about what would happen to his dog until now, and wondered if Patrick would look after him.

"We met her outside a shop. She's a bit of a crisp and chocolate addict, apparently, and while we were trying to stop Dad from buying another Fudge, she came out and we invited her."

"No, don't say that word. Too late," sighed Uncle Ernie in a panic. "Now I'll never get that theme tune out of my head."

"It's a real earworm, that's for sure," I laughed. "I've been humming it for the past hour without even realising. Anyway, we invited her. Does she know Patrick, I wonder?"

"Patrick's a local, so maybe. They seem quite friendly."

"At least she has someone to talk to. She was reticent about coming."

"You can't blame her. This isn't exactly a conventional party." Uncle Ernie heaved to his feet, tidied away his plate, then stood before us and said, "Time for some live music, I think. I'll round up the guys, then we'll do a few songs, get things really going, and then I'm done for the evening and can relax."

"Knock 'em dead, Ernie," encouraged Dad.

"Break a leg," giggled Mum, who might have drunk her wine too rapidly.

Uncle Ernie walked over to his bandmates in his usual manner. As if it was urgent, his skinny legs pumping, arms swinging back and forth, elbows sticking out. I had to smile. It was hard to pinpoint, but everything about him screamed ska. The slightly manic yet also relaxed and chilled movements, combining a mellow vibe with a sense of urgency, just like his music. He looked awesome in his wedding clothes, and so did Freya, and as the band set up and people gathered around, we went over to watch.

"It's an acoustic set today," Uncle Ernie informed everyone. "Nobody wants to be lugging amps and gear onto the beach, but we're still going to blow you away!"

Everyone cheered, Uncle Ernie took a bow, then the guitarist jumped straight into it, the rhythm joined by the drummer, then the sax. When Uncle Ernie sang it could have been like any other concert, if not for the dogs that began to howl as the music soared and people swayed to the beat.

The guys really went for it, the soaring vocals of fast, rap-like lyrics encouraging everyone to dance. With wild bursts of punk interspersed with mellow sections, it was timed perfectly and I kept forgetting this was done with no microphones or speakers. Just musicians who had been playing almost their entire lives and knew their instruments better than they knew anything else.

My kind-hearted uncle dedicated the next song to his new wife, and she raced over to hug him before dancing with her sister, who went wild. Maybe it was the grief, the shock wearing off, or the sense of freedom at no longer being tied to a man she had no love for, but whatever it was she seemed to become something else and flung herself around the sand with wild abandon, causing everyone else to copy her. Soon, the beach was awash with bodies flinging themselves about in one giant release of pent-up energy the likes of which I'd never seen before.

Mum and Dad were doing things in their own way as usual, Mum twirling her dress as Dad spun her around, then jiving before morphing into a skank and striking poses with earnest dedication.

I moved away a little to watch, eyes wandering over the faces of the people, noting how they acted, who they were focused on, or who seemed too excited. Others appeared sad and deflated, watching from the side rather than joining in.

It certainly wasn't all joyful as I'd first believed when otherwise pre-occupied. Sure, most guests were having fun, but for some it was rather forced, their facial expressions belying how they were acting. Others made no bones about the fact that the day had been far from perfect, and many were clearly unhappy with aspects of it. You could hardly blame them. Deaths, police, timings gone wrong, upset owners, rampaging dogs, and missed meal times. It had all happened, and clearly rankled.

Quite a few guests were merely sipping drinks and watching, either not party people or too tired from the day. Many dogs were clearly overwhelmed, too, and were sitting with their owners or fast asleep. I got the impression that for some the entire event had been a letdown and not what they'd expected at all.

Those with sour faces were mostly ones I recalled having been the most argumentative about how their dog's wedding should be organised. Insisting on different music, different confetti, different treats to be given, and endless requests, not all of which could be fulfilled. I didn't envy Freya and Susie one bit. I assumed this was why they mostly did single weddings rather than group ones, as dealing with so many people was nothing but a headache and left plenty of them disappointed.

But as I took stock of things, it was evident that overall they had done an excellent job of giving people what they wanted and recovering from what'd been a truly terrible start to the day.

"Are you not dancing, Rachel?" I asked as I joined her by the bar where she was gulping wine and rather red-faced.

"Do I look like I am?" she snapped, finishing her drink.

"Sorry to intrude," I said, then made to leave.

"No, don't go! Max, I apologise. I'm tipsy, and it's been an exhausting day. I wanted to come to support my best friend, but it was a long drive early this morning. Freya's been great, but a real handful because of the stress, and with the deaths it's just been too much. How can they both be so happy when Neil is dead, one of their clients jumped off a building, and the day was such a mess?"

"It's their way of coping with things. Remember, Freya got married, and loves Uncle Ernie, so she's happy. Sure, she's upset for her sister, but she's got a new future to look forward to."

"With him." Rachel focused on Uncle Ernie who was belting out one of their hits, pacing back and forth like he was playing Glastonbury not a wedding party.

"You're still concerned about losing her, aren't you?"

"Not really. I know things will never be the same again. It doesn't matter what she says. She'll always be there for me, but it can't be the same. How could it be?"

"You're right. I won't deny that. Things change. That's what life is like. But you have a best friend and someone who cares for you very much, and that's more than most people can say. Be happy for them."

"I'm trying to be, Max, I really am. But it's hard. She's all I've got and now it's been taken away from me. Susie kept encouraging her to marry him, and she listens to her sister. Well, Susie isn't so great, and now she's lost her own husband. An eye for an eye."

"What do you mean?"

"Nothing. I, er, I think I've had one too many. Excuse me." Rachel rushed off and called for Two-tone who was with Anxious and Special down by the water, racing around playing dodge the water as they barked and ran up the beach every time a wave rolled in.

She was clearly more upset than I'd imagined about her best friend marrying Uncle Ernie, and once again I considered the possibility that she'd done something to Neil to try to ruin the event. Was that what she meant by an eye for an eye? Susie took her friend away by encouraging her to get married, so she killed her husband? Or maybe she meant nothing by it. People say all sorts when under the influence. Or was it that the drink had made her tell the truth?

I spied Amy walking towards the shoreline with Patrick, his dog by his side, the Chihuahua still asleep in his arms. They were very serious, heads close together, and yet kept glancing around to ensure nobody was near. If anyone passed, they stopped talking, then resumed when alone again. Maybe Patrick had been the one to do this? What if he'd had enough of Marcus and his ways and had done the deed? But why kill Neil?

Then I got completely carried away and even considered that Amy, a woman charged with saving lives, could have somehow been involved in this. Maybe she knew the dead men? Not likely as neither lived locally, but still possible. Or was there another motive and they were just the innocent victims because of her plans? What might those be beyond what'd already been considered? To disrupt the event and give the women's business a bad name? I was definitely overthinking this, but something was nagging at me and becoming more insistent. Something wasn't right about any of this and I was getting closer.

Anxious ran over to me, tongue lolling, panting happily. Two-tone was with Rachel who had dropped to the wet sand and was making a fuss of the equally exhausted dog. Special had returned to Freya and was running around her and Susie while they danced.

I sat on the sand beside Anxious and asked, "Have you had a good time?"

A happy bark was the answer.

"Do we think someone here was responsible?"

Anxious barked, tail wagging, but then the strangest thing happened. He turned, locked his eyes on mine, and with his tail still, which it never was, he barked again.

"Are you saying it wasn't someone who was here?"

A single bark.

"Do you mean yes for one bark?"

Anxious barked three times!

I laughed, then hugged the little guy, who responded by licking my beard and then jumping up and running over to a group of dogs to ask if he could play. I shook my head as I smiled at my own foolishness. Over the years, I'd begun to believe Anxious could understand everything that was said and everything that was going on around him. Maybe not believe, maybe wanted him to would be more accurate.

Sure, he was smart, and did pick up on more than any other dog I had ever known, but however hard I'd tried we didn't have an infallible system for him answering me. I'd tried the one bark for yes, two barks for no, and sometimes it had worked, other times not. Most likely, it was nothing more than wishful thinking on my part. He did understand an awful lot, so maybe my expectations had grown too high. Or maybe he was right and the killer wasn't anyone present. If not, then that opened up a whole other can of worms. It meant I had absolutely no idea what the motive could have been.

But then something hit me, and I could have slapped myself if I was a violent man. I did have an idea as to motive, and it had been staring me in the face the whole time. How could I have been so blind? It was obvious now I thought about it, and surely this had to be the answer to at least part of this mystery.

But there was one big issue with all of this. Even if I knew the motive, how on earth were these two despicable acts carried out? This had been the main problem from the very start, but I think I finally had the answer as I watched dogs play and people dance.

Yes, I had an explanation I believed was actually possible. Proving it would be another matter entirely.

I'd find a way. With a little help from family and friends.

Chapter 17

The Skankin' Skeletons might not have been dressed in their usual outfits and had foregone the makeup, but that in no way hindered their ability to rock a party. The guys were giving it their all. If anything, they seemed to be more energetic than ever. Maybe it was the fact they had to deal with no sound system, or because Uncle Ernie was so upbeat, buzzing off his marriage to the love of his life, that his mood was contagious. Maybe it was the incredible venue. How often did a band get to play on a beach with such a captive audience?

Whatever it was, the manic energy had spread through the crowd and the dancing grew increasingly wild. But as the beat intensified and the skanking turned almost violent when a mosh pit formed, others grew more sullen. Rachel was now standing at the top of the beach, continually glancing at Freya and Susie as they threw their arms around with wild abandon. Amy and Patrick had parted ways, and Amy now seemed at a loss as to what to do so simply watched the frenzied activity with her mouth turned down.

Patrick still cradled Marcus' dog, shaking his head now and then as he observed the dancing impassively. Several other people were clearly beyond bored and would have left if they had a choice, but had to wait for the coach to take them back to the hotel.

Small groups had formed, with people clearly grumbling about the way the event had turned out. Either they weren't party people, or hated ska. How could anyone hate ska? I took my time studying everyone and everything, letting it all soak in and help to give me the full picture of this peculiar day. Several guests simply upped and left, and it wasn't just those with their own cars. I noted a few individuals crossing the car park then heading back into the city centre on foot. After all, it was probably only a thirty-minute walk at most, and the road would be quiet at this time of the evening.

Ideally, everyone would have remained together, but I knew that was impossible, and besides, it wasn't really necessary. The main players were mostly all here, and that was the main thing. But for how long, and would that be enough to get this mystery solved?

Deciding to give myself a break from the mental gymnastics, I put my worries aside and joined the others on the sand for a dance. I let myself go crazy, lost to the music, and soon worked up a considerable sweat as I skanked, the rhythm pounding through my bones, my arms and legs acting of their own volition. Carefree, and not thinking about anything at all. When the band performed an astonishing cover of Sublime's *What I Got*, I became truly euphoric.

The tempo upped as the guys played their final tune, sending the revellers to new heights of wild abandon, and I was one of them. We became a single entity, caught up in the atmosphere and feeding off the group energy. I was almost overwhelmed by the intensity of the emotion it evoked. Losing myself to the communal buzz was not something that'd happened to me in quite such a deep way before, and it was almost scary. But I went with it, welcomed the release, and had so much fun I was rather shocked when the last chord was struck and the music died, leaving me grinning like the others as we emerged from our trance and stared at each other, feeling the bond the music had created and knowing we were better people because of it.

"That was incredible!" gushed Susie, face flushed, eyes wild, hair plastered to her head as she rather unexpectedly hugged me, then Freya, then Mum and Dad.

"Amazing," I agreed, finding it hard to talk as I was smiling so much because of the adrenaline.

"My man is the best!" roared Freya, glancing at her husband as he spoke animatedly with his bandmates.

"Best gig ever," said Dad, then hugged Mum who was wobbly from the exertion.

"Let's get a drink," croaked Mum, then took Dad's arm and we moved over to the bar where plenty of others were already helping themselves to the various offerings.

The band came over, their sweaty faces gleaming as the slowly setting sun cast an orange glow over us.

"How was it?" asked Uncle Ernie as the DJ played The Royals' *Pick Up The Pieces* so the vibe could change to chilled summer evening for the rest of the party.

"We thought you were incredible," I said. "Amazing, in fact. You did so well, and you'd never even know it was an acoustic set."

"Thanks, everyone. We felt such a deep connection with each other and the audience, and we might have gone a little crazy." Uncle Ernie gulped a bottle of water then grabbed a beer and we all clinked glasses and bottles, unable to stop smiling, knowing this had been a truly special evening.

"You did us all proud, my love," said Freya, kissing him, which made his smile spread wider.

"Yes, thank you so much," said Susie, her eyes still wild, clearly not coming down from the high yet.

The band thanked Susie, and she thanked them again, but it was obvious she was far from right. She began to shake, then her eyes rolled up as she went limp.

Dad caught her before she hit the sand; she went rigid a moment later as her eyes snapped open. Susie flailed at him until she regained her senses, then coughed, pulled away as he released her, and looked at us in shock.

"Sorry. So sorry. What happened?" she stammered, wiping her face repeatedly in a manic manner, eyes roaming.

"You had a bit of a turn, love," said Dad softly. "Maybe you should call it a day, eh?"

"No, I… I'm fine. Just danced too much. I'll rest, but I'm okay."

"I think she should go home," Mum told Freya.

"That's a good idea. Come on, Susie, let's get you back to the hotel." Freya held her hand out for Susie, but she shook her head.

"No, I want to stay. We have to ensure our guests enjoys themselves, and the party isn't over yet. We haven't even done the cakes. Can someone go and get them?"

"Are you sure, love?" asked Dad. "I've seen this before. You overdid it, and you're exhausted. Too much has happened today. You should get some sleep."

"I don't want to sleep! How could I? I want to make this the best wedding ever. I know it's been awful, but we have to do the cake."

Freya took Susie off to one side and tried to convince her that she'd had enough, but it was clear Susie was insisting on staying. Susie shook her head and turned, then hurried back to us with Freya on her heels, but as Susie approached she lost her frown, and when Freya caught her up she hugged her sister then said, "I'm so sorry, everyone. I didn't want to cause a scene. I'm absolutely fine. You're right, it's been a very long, tiring, upsetting day and I shouldn't be so pig-headed. Let's finish the party off with cake and drinks, then I'm sure people will be happy to leave anyway. Does that sound alright?"

We agreed that it sounded perfect as long as she was up to it, so Freya and Susie organised the staff now the barbecue had been cleared away and it was time for the cakes. Freya asked if Uncle Ernie and I could go and get them, so with Dad enlisted, too, we headed up to the work van and opened up the back.

"Blimey, they're huge," gasped Dad as we were confronted with the two cakes.

"Freya and Susie like to go big," laughed Uncle Ernie. "The one for the dogs is a special recipe, and Susie always makes them. They both made our wedding cake."

"They don't buy them in?" I asked.

"Max, they cost an absolute fortune from a professional. They save literally hundreds by doing it themselves. This is why they're so successful. They put the work in and reap the rewards. I'm proud of them both."

"Susie had a wobble back there, but she seems okay now," noted Dad as he folded over his sleeves so his biceps bulged. "But these guns can handle the cakes. I'll take your one, Ernie, you two bring the one for the dogs. Wow, they're gonna love this."

Dad hefted the large cake, winking at me as veins popped on his arms, then Uncle Ernie and I carefully eased the other massive three-tier cake from the van.

"It weighs a ton," I laughed. "Think we'll make it without dropping it?"

"We better, or the sisters will give us what for," chuckled Uncle Ernie, the strain evident on his face.

"Let's hope nobody has poisoned them," chortled Dad.

"Why would you say that?" I asked, intrigued, things popping in my head like miniature lightbulbs being switched on.

"I'm not sure," he said, frowning. "Just after the murders and us not solving them yet, I wondered if the killer was still out to get other people."

"Guys, I'm coming around to the idea that they were accidents, nothing more," said Uncle Ernie. "It seems kind of surreal already. Like it didn't happen. Does that make sense?"

"Sure it does," said Dad. "But they were murdered, that's for sure."

"How do you know?" asked Uncle Ernie.

"Because of the fact two men jumped in one day and everyone agreed neither was the sort to do it voluntarily. They weren't unhappy enough. No, it was murder alright. I know nobody really liked either of them, but they still deserve justice. Max, what do you think?"

"It was definitely murder."

"But how?" asked Uncle Ernie.

"I think we're going to find out soon enough, but first let's get these cakes down to the beach before we drop them."

Carefully, we made the short walk. Dad stormed ahead, trying to get a pump in his arms and show off, but he began to flag and soon was almost bent over under the weight but refused the offers of assistance as everyone gathered around as we approached.

Uncle Ernie and I didn't fare much better, and our difference in height meant I had to stoop to keep the cake level, and my back began to ache terribly.

We placed them on the table to a loud round of applause and plenty of kind words for Susie and Freya, then we stood back so the two sisters could stand in front of their hard work and say a few words. Uncle Ernie joined them, and was the first to speak, thanking everyone for coming and telling us how happy he was to have Freya as his wife. He kept it short, which was unusual for him, but he wanted the sisters to get the credit they deserved for soldiering on through what had been a very difficult time, especially for Susie.

Once Susie and Freya had given very brief speeches, skirting around the deaths, they explained that there would be cake and drinks, then the coach would take people back to their hotels and campsites.

After a raucous round of applause, Freya cut into the cake for the dogs. Like blood to a shark, the ravenous pooches came tearing from their various positions on the beach, drawn by the scents of dog food, their hunger from the exercise evident by the amount of drool soaking into the dry sand.

We set up a human chain with the plates and handed them to the owners who then took their dogs away so others could get theirs, and soon enough the cake was devoured. Then it was time for the star of the show.

The glossy, three-tier wedding cake was decorated with miniature clones of Freya and Uncle Ernie in their wedding finery, which Freya removed and carefully stored in a container. With broad grins, the happy couple held the knife together and cut into the cake. Everyone applauded, numerous photos were taken, then we repeated the human chain and those who wanted some were given their cake.

I felt nervous about everyone eating it, but then shook it off as paranoia and bit into the delicious-looking cake along with everyone else.

For a moment I was wracked with confusion, and the silence meant I wasn't the only one. I chewed again, but something was definitely wrong. Was I right after all? Was Dad? Had the cake been tampered with? Was this to be a mass killing the likes of which the country had never seen?

"Gross!" someone shouted.

"It tastes weird," said Dad, licking his lips, his face twisted in a grimace.

"It's dog food," I sighed, then spat out the cake onto my plate and wiped my face with a napkin.

"I'm poisoned," wailed Mum, spitting hers onto Dad's plate then grabbing his immaculate T-shirt and yanking it up to wipe her mouth.

"Oi! Geddof! What are you doing, you daft fool? It's not poison, it's dog food." Dad took Mum's hand and prised her fingers from his now filthy top then smoothed it down, but it was ruined, and he wasn't happy.

"Sorry, I panicked. Why is it dog food?"

As everyone else grumbled, all eyes turned to Freya and Susie who were utterly mortified and rooted to the spot, staring at each other in confusion.

"We didn't get them mixed up, did we? I thought the one with the models on was the cake for people? We kept them separate and made the doggie cake the day before. How did this happen?" asked Freya.

"I don't know!" wailed Susie, sinking to her knees and beating at the sand with her fists. "Someone did this. It's all linked. They murdered my husband, then Marcus, and switched the cakes. It's a conspiracy. They're trying to ruin us." Susie shot up and glared at the shocked guests. "Who was it? Who did this? Why are you out to destroy us? It's sick! You killed my husband and now you ruined my sister's wedding cake. It's despicable." Susie ran off up the beach towards the car park, unable to cope with it any longer.

The stunned guests began to shift uncomfortably and talk amongst themselves, but I caught sight of Rachel and noted the smirk that twitched her lips before she caught my eye and the smile vanished.

Amy came over and asked, "Are their weddings usually like this? It's very intense, isn't it? Corpses, cakes, and utter confusion. It's enough to make your head spin. I think I'd like to go home now. Do you mind?"

"No, not at all. I think it's time for everyone to leave. Can you give me five minutes to help sort things out here, then we'll be off?"

"Of course. Actually, no, it doesn't matter. Patrick said he was heading home soon, so maybe I'll go back with him. He's local."

"If you're sure?"

"Yes, it's fine, Max. Don't worry. Um, thanks for the invite, but next time, I think I'll pass on the party." Amy smiled to show she was joking, but who could blame her if she wasn't? She joined Patrick, who nodded, then with

Buttercup still asleep in his arms and the Poodle by his side, he left with Amy.

Most other people hurried up the beach, too, and cars began to leave. The DJ packed up his things and with the help of the staff hauled the gear to the car park while I busied myself gathering dropped plates and bagging any cake that the dogs hadn't managed to snaffle in the confusion. No wonder they ate theirs so fast. I hoped there was nothing to upset their stomachs in it, as usually wedding cakes were very rich and there sure was a lot of icing.

Mum and Dad pitched in, Uncle Ernie consoled Freya as they gathered up cups and loaded the remaining drinks into boxes or crates, and the staff said their goodbyes as they took everything up to the van before they went home after a long day's work Freya made a point of thanking them for. Soon everyone had left apart from me and the folks, Uncle Ernie, Freya, and Rachel. Susie still hadn't made an appearance after storming off, and I doubted she would return to the beach.

Anxious stared at me with his head cocked, and I knew what he was thinking. I bent and whispered, "Not yet, buddy. I don't think it's time for treats now, do you? Not after that cake."

He disagreed and barked, then checked on my pocket, but I held my ground even though his behaviour had been impeccable through a very trying day.

"What now?" asked Dad.

"Now we get out of here and hope we aren't murdered in our beds," said Mum cheerily.

"What are you so happy about?" I asked.

"Obvious, isn't it?" she asked, frowning.

"Not to me."

"Or me," agreed Dad.

"Or me," said Uncle Ernie.

Rachel and Freya remained silent.

"It means the killer was here. Which means Max knows who it is. Isn't that right?"

"Mum, now's not the time," I insisted. "And anyway, I don't know."

"You don't?" Her disappointment was evident.

"No, but I've got an inkling."

"Ooh, did you hear that, love?" gushed Mum to Dad. "He's got an inkling. I adore it when he inks."

"You don't ink," sighed Dad, shaking his head.

"You don't? What's it called when you have an inkling then? You must ink to have one."

"It's just inkling. That's it. Come on, time to go."

We agreed, so returned to the now almost empty car park where just the campervan and work van remained. Susie was leaning against the back, eyes red and face blotchy, but her tears had dried and what remained was a look of unparalleled anger.

"They can kill my husband, try to ruin my business, but nobody, absolutely nobody, messes with my sister's happiness. I'm going to destroy whoever did this," she hissed, fists clenched tight.

"It's alright," soothed Freya. "We still had a lovely wedding. Right, Ernie?"

"Er, yes, absolutely. It's been chaotic, mad, and upsetting for you especially, Susie, but the main things is Freya and I are married."

"You call that a lovely day?" asked Rachel. "It's been a disaster. It's not a good sign for the future."

"Who cares what happened to the cakes?" said Freya. "And Rachel, please don't infer that our future is doomed. That's not what best friends do."

Rachel reddened, but said nothing. Uncle Ernie and I exchanged a knowing look. No words were needed, but we both knew who'd switched the cakes.

We left after promising to meet up tomorrow when hopefully a new day would bring better news for everyone, or at least no more bad news.

Chapter 18

I slept amazingly well, and after coffee I made a call to Amy because something she'd said was niggling me. She was surprised to hear from me, but was happy enough to answer my very early morning questions. Her shift began at seven so the conversation was relatively brief, but what she did promise to do was meet at the Bishop's Palace at nine if possible.

Next, I called Uncle Ernie and explained to him what was going on. Although I hated to do it to him on the first day of his honeymoon, he readily agreed to round up everyone else and meet me there too.

I'd already arranged to have an early breakfast at eight with Mum and Dad, so got myself ready then headed into the miniature city and parked in the usual car park, planning to meet them on the high street at a charming cafe I'd spotted yesterday.

I grinned as I pulled into the space, spying Dubman's more modern, but still classic, campervan directly opposite me. He was just exiting, so I got out with Anxious and waved. He crossed over and came to join us, so we moved onto the grass out of the way.

"We meet yet again," I laughed.

"It's becoming a habit," he agreed with a warm smile and a firm handshake. "What brings you into this great little city so early on a Sunday? After yesterday, I figured you'd be sleeping in."

"It's a long story. And it's a shame you didn't stay for the party yesterday. We had a great time, even if the ending was upsetting for Freya and Susie."

"Do tell," he said with an eager grin, clearly a man who liked to hear the gossip.

I don't know what came over me, and I was never usually like this with strangers, but something about Dubman made me certain I could trust him. Maybe it was Anxious' friendly nature towards him, his relaxed attitude, the general chilled vibe, or possibly because he was a fellow VW owner, but without even realising, I began with the story of the cakes then backtracked and told him the whole sorry tale. I even imparted who I believed killed the two men, and the moment I did, he grew serious.

"That whole family had a rough time of it the last few years. The dad died, but then there was a terrible business and the mum passed."

"What happened? How do you know?"

"I'm a chatty guy, and get to hear all the gossip. Plus, I know everyone. This is my hometown and people love to chat around here. Didn't I say?"

"No. I figured you were passing through."

"I am, kind of. I'm staying in my van, but came home to visit my Mum."

"So what do you know about the family?"

Dubman went on to explain what he'd heard through the gossip grapevine, and it made me even more convinced that I was right and my suspicions were correct. I laid out my plan, and he was hopping with excitement once I'd finished.

"I can help. Listen, you aren't going to just get them to admit any of this. You need a way to get them to confess. I think I have the perfect solution."

He explained his idea, and I absolutely refused, but he swayed me by insisting that he'd grown up here and knew the ruins like the back of his hand. He promised he'd be able to help get a confession by performing a slight act of subterfuge, and eventually he won me over with his winning smile and conviction.

We agreed to meet soon, but he had a few errands to run first so Anxious and I hurried to meet my folks who were sipping coffees and bickering happily in their usual animated way.

"Max, tell your mother that it absolutely is not normal to enjoy cake made for dogs. She reckons she's going to make it and we'll have it every Sunday. She's gone mad in the head. Skull full of rocks, this one. I think she needs a doctor."

"Um, morning." I kissed Mum, hugged Dad, then sat.

"Morning, love," beamed Mum.

Anxious got a fuss and a sneaky biscuit Mum thought I didn't see, then I asked, "What's this about cake? You didn't actually enjoy it, did you?"

"What if I did? Freya said the food they used was suitable for human consumption and nobody would get ill. I liked the crunch. I told your father that I'm going to make it, as apparently it's full of antioxidants and it might improve the sheen of our hair. It works wonders for dogs' coats, so I'm willing to give it a try." Mum winked at me and tried to keep a straight face as Dad performed an emergency hair comb.

"My hair's lustrous enough, and yours is always so glossy, love. Mind you, I wouldn't go near it with a naked flame, the amount of hairspray you use, but we don't need any more shine. Max, tell her. I can't have my Sunday dinner ruined."

Mum and I burst out laughing as she wagged a finger in his face and teased, "You daft lump! Of course I'm not going to ruin Sunday dinner. It's sacred."

"Phew. So you were joking around?"

"Yes. We'll have it on Veggie Tuesday instead. You always complain when there's no meat, so now you'll get some extra protein."

Dad smiled, but it faded when Mum remained serious. He turned to me, eyes imploring, but I shook my head. When he faced Mum, she was fit to bursting, and he sighed with relief.

"Now, let me fill you in on what's about to happen. I hope you're both ready for some real intrigue, and to help solve this puzzling mystery?"

"Oh, goodie." Mum clapped her hands together and Dad leaned forward, hands cupped to his ears so he didn't miss a single word.

Breakfast was served partway through my explanation, but nobody even lifted a piece of toast until I'd finished going over things. I leaned back and smiled at them once I'd summed everything up, then bit into a sausage as they stared at me until it became uncomfortable.

"What?"

"We thought we were going to solve it," pouted Mum, pulling her bandanna—red and black to match today's dress—low to her eyes.

"We were sure we had it figured out. We were up half the night talking about things and were certain who the killer was. Neither of us knew how they did it, but I was confident we had our culprit."

"We didn't even have any nooky as we were too tired after all the thinking," complained Mum.

"No, do not even go there. I do not want to be thinking about you two getting it on while I have my breakfast." I eyed my sausage warily, then sighed as I put it back on the plate.

"Max, you know we still have a very active love life and at least twice a week we like to get—"

"Stop!" I warned, feeling light-headed.

"He's such a prude." Dad shook his head, as if disappointed in me, and Mum did the same.

"Can we please get back to the subject of murder? It's much less upsetting."

"What can we do to help?" asked Mum, perking up.

"Okay, so here's the plan."

We went over things while we ate, although Dad had my remaining sausage. Once finished, we had to hurry down the street and over to the Bishop's Palace where some of the others had already arrived and I spied the rest coming along the path.

Uncle Ernie and Freya were holding hands at the main entrance, reliving yesterday's vows judging by the smiles on their faces. Susie and Rachel were walking around to the east wing, presumably so Susie could take a look at where her husband fell.

Dubman was swaggering towards them, smiling as he said hello, and as we approached everyone stopped what they were doing and we grouped together at the spot where Neil had lost his life.

Everyone began asking questions at once, but as I spied the last of our guests to arrive, Dubman disappeared after I nodded to him.

Anxious, Special, and Two-tone had a quick sniff hello then ran around a little, but I could tell by Anxious' movements that he was just being polite and a moment later he returned and sat by my side.

"Please just bear with me for a while. I promise everything will make sense soon. Nobody do anything rash, and remain calm. Susie, I know this is difficult for you, but I also know you want answers. You asked me to get them, so that's exactly what I'm going to do, okay?"

"Okay," she agreed, glancing at the wall then turning away.

Rachel's eyes roamed continually, looking like this was the last place on earth she wanted to be, and Freya had lost her good humour and was hanging on to Uncle Ernie as if she couldn't support her own weight.

Amy called out a loud hello, so we greeted her and a very confused-looking Peter who was fishing around in a pack of crisps which he then upended before stuffing the wrapper into his paramedic's high vis jacket, the pocket bulging.

"Thanks for coming," I told her.

"What's this about?" Peter frowned as he took in our small group.

"I told you, Max wanted to have a word and I said I'd come if we weren't on a call. You don't mind, do you?"

"Um, I guess not. Hi, Max. And, um, hi to everyone else."

"Hi," I said brightly. "Peter, sorry to be a bother, but it's good to see you again. How did the fishing go yesterday?"

"Amazing! Caught more than you, I think," he laughed, relaxing.

"Great job. Now, I know it's strange meeting like this, especially here, but I wanted the main people involved in what happened to be present."

"Then why are we here?" asked Amy.

"Because you and Peter were so kind to Susie and everyone else, and were on the scene before the police both times, so it's important that you be here," I explained.

"But we weren't involved," added Peter. "We just helped as best we could, but it was too little, too late."

"Or was it?" I asked.

Mum let out a little gasp, but I silenced her with a look then turned back to Peter.

"How'd you mean?"

"I mean, something about it has been bugging me, and it's only recently that it started to make sense." I took a step back so everyone could see me properly, and Anxious did the same. "It was a big coincidence that both Freya and

Susie were nowhere to be seen when both men jumped. Then you appeared a moment later, looking flushed, and I have to admit, very guilty. Rachel, you said you arrived a while later, but nobody saw when. You could have been on the scene for ages, no matter what you said."

"Are you saying we did it?" asked Rachel, eyes flashing dark.

"No, I'm just explaining how I came to the conclusion I did. When Amy and Peter arrived, Amy was kind enough to move Neil so you could recover a little, Susie, but there was something off about the whole thing."

"What was that?" asked Uncle Ernie.

"That Peter seemed to recognise you, Susie."

"I'd never met her before yesterday," said Peter with a frown.

"That's right. We never met before," agreed Susie.

"No, but what if he still recognised you?"

"From the news or something?" she asked. "Or because of the business?"

"Most likely from the news. And it was the same with Marcus. Peter, did you know those men?" I tried to keep my tone light, but as everyone focused on Peter and he glanced from me to Amy, then the others, it was clear he was being put on the spot.

"How would I? They weren't from around here."

"No, but they'd both had business here. Maybe not in person, but I think you did know who they were. Tell me something, Peter. Do you really believe that because Neil fell to his death, Marcus was a copycat and decided to jump as well?"

"It's the only explanation, isn't it? What other reason can there be?"

"You know exactly what the reason is. I think you knew both men, and I'm convinced you killed them."

Everyone gasped and focused their attention on Peter.

"I thought you were a good guy, Max, but you've obviously got a screw loose. Is this a sick, twisted joke? You're off your rocker, mate. I thought we'd got on yesterday?"

"We did, but now things are different. Now I'm certain it was you who killed them, and that's why you were so quick on the scene. You hung around close by on purpose to be sure you could be the first to arrive and check they were dead. Maybe if they'd lived, you'd have bundled them into the ambulance and ensured they died before they reached the hospital."

"That's nuts. You're off your head. Amy, are you in on this? Did you trick me into coming?"

"You have to admit what you did, Peter," said Amy sadly. "People might start using this place as somewhere to end their lives, and that would be awful. Do you want that on your conscience?"

"No, of course not! But I didn't do it. How could I have?"

"Because you were out of the ambulance and had disappeared when they died, then returned just in time to get the call. It's awful what you did, and you have to own up. You lied, and you killed."

"I've heard enough. I'm outta here."

Peter turned to leave, but a shout from high on the gable wall gave him pause, and he turned along with the rest of us to see who was shouting.

Chapter 19

"I can't take it any more," hollered Dubman from the top of the wall. He teetered, and my heart leapt into my mouth. The last thing I wanted was for him to die as well. But he seemed to know what he was doing, and leaned back and grabbed the wall to steady himself as everyone cried out for him to get down.

"No, this wasn't supposed to happen," stammered Peter, almost too quietly for me to hear.

"What wasn't supposed to happen, Peter?" I asked loudly, causing everyone to focus on us.

"Nothing. I was just worried that Dubman might fall. Why is he doing this?"

"Why would anyone jump?" I asked.

"How would I know? Look, you can't seriously believe I'm to blame for any of this. Amy, why did you trick me?"

"I think you know why. Max explained everything this morning, and it made sense. You were acting strangely yesterday. You kept saying I disappeared and took ages going to the shop or the toilet, but I knew I was right and you were the one who'd vanished. You weren't waiting where I'd left you, but you insisted I'd got the wrong location. I was exhausted and thought you were right, but you weren't. You lied."

"What are you talking about? You've all gone soft in the head. I'm leaving." Peter spun sharply, but Anxious growled as he planted himself firmly in his way, the rest of us behind him facing Peter.

"He'll bite you if you try," I explained.

"He better not. I love dogs, but I'm going to defend myself."

"And kill again, like you already have?" asked Mum, the excitement in her voice evident. Plus, she was smiling.

"Kill? Me? You really are nuts. Get that mutt out of my way." Peter took a short step but Anxious was having none of it and growled from deep in his belly, causing Peter to pause.

"You did it, and I know how," I explained.

"Go on then, tell me. Those men obviously jumped, but please, explain how I pushed them even though nobody was up there with them?"

"That's where you're wrong. We didn't see you because of the height. If you were behind them but on a lower level, nobody would have noticed anything. You shoved at their legs and they fell."

"Nonsense. Utter rubbish. You're making this up to get a rise out of me. I don't know why, but you've got it in for me. What did I ever do to you, eh? Nothing, that's what."

"No, nothing to me, but what about the men who ruined your mother's life?"

Peter gasped and staggered backwards, eyes darting, but then he threw his head back and laughed, his neck flushing. "You're desperate to pin this on me, aren't you? For your information, my mum's dead. Has been for a few years. Amy, did you tell him?"

"I did, once Max told me that he suspected you but wasn't sure of the reason why, although he had a very good idea. Peter, tell me this isn't true. Why would you do such a horrid thing? You'll go to prison. You destroyed your whole life for revenge?"

"They deserved it," he spat, eyes widening in shock before a sly smile spread across his face and he laughed again. "Maybe Neil and Marcus did destroy my mum's business, and maybe she did collapse with a heart attack when she went bankrupt, leaving me without a mother, but that doesn't prove anything. Where's your proof, eh?" he taunted, eyes boring into me with boiling hate.

"Catch," I warned, then threw the item from my pocket at him.

Acting on instinct, he grabbed it then frowned as he asked, "A pack of crisps? I don't get it."

"You're always eating them. Cheese and onion flavour specifically. Amy said too much junk food is an issue for both of you, and you've gained weight recently because you refuse to eat healthily."

"I'm the same," she said. "We're always on the go and grab meal deals from the supermarkets mostly. But Peter, you go through so many packs of crisps every day. Your pockets are always full of them, and you're always dropping the wrappers."

"So what? It's nobody else's business."

"But you left your empty packet up on the parapet," I explained. "The detective, and us, thought nothing of it, and he closed the case without even checking for fingerprints. But last night I got him to run your prints, which Amy provided from a cup in the ambulance you use, and guess whose showed up on the litter you left up there along with your water bottle? You were up there, waiting, eating a late breakfast, or early lunch, and when Neil met you on the parapet you got him onto the wall then pushed him off."

"So what if my prints were on the packet? That proves nothing. I like to go up there some days and look at the view. It's stunning."

"But it gets cleared away every day, so this proves you were up there yesterday right before he fell. Admit it, Peter. You killed them both." I knew I was taking a risk lying about the fingerprints, but as he balked I relaxed; he was close to admitting things now.

"Liar! Amy, you know me," he pleaded. "Tell them I wouldn't hurt anyone."

"That's what I told Max, but when he explained why he thought you'd done it, I had to be sure. Now I am. You did it, and then you had the nerve to tell me off for wanting to save poor Susie from seeing her husband like that."

"Fingerprints aren't proof," insisted Peter, but he was sweating more than he should have and was clearly ready to bolt. Anxious sensed this and growled again, but Peter was oblivious now, lost to his own whirling thoughts.

"Admit it, son," said Dad. "We know you did it. If those men ruined your mum's business and you blamed them for her death, it's obviously a motive. With the fingerprints, you'll be arrested soon enough and go to trial. They'll find you guilty, so you may as well own up and make it easier for yourself. How'd you get them up there, eh? What did you do?"

"Fine! Yes, I killed them, and they deserved worse. They killed my mum and didn't care. Just faceless nobody's who destroyed everything she'd worked for with one stroke of a pen. I hated them and knew I had my chance when I heard about the wedding. I got Neil to come by telling him I had proof he was having an affair. Guess it worked, so sorry about that," he told Susie.

"He swore he would never do that again," she murmured, so shocked she hadn't even reacted to Peter's admission until now.

"Yeah, well, he was a bad guy, wasn't he? I read about his last affair and knew he was the kind of man who would do it again. I told him to meet me up on the parapet and he'd better get Mum's ring and give it to me. She'd sold it off years ago to try to provide for us, but it wasn't enough.

It was still in the pawn shop, so he bought it back and met me to hand it over. He showed it to me as proof, and I smacked it out of his hand. When he climbed up to get it, I shoved him and he fell. There, is that what you wanted to hear?"

"Not cool, dude. Not cool at all," tutted Dubman as he appeared beside me then nodded a hello to everyone. I nodded back and mouthed a silent thank you for the part he played, then focused on Peter.

"You tricked him into meeting you, then shoved him off and climbed back down and returned to the ambulance like nothing happened?" asked Uncle Ernie. "That's cold."

"Not as cold as he was!" hissed Peter. He spoke directly to Susie when he said, "He didn't even care about you finding out. Said he'd talk you around, and you were weak and would forgive him again. He was just worried about it getting into the papers and his boss finding out. Said he might lose his job if there was another scandal. I insisted on seeing the ring before I gave him the proof, and then he only cared about the ring and how much it cost. Dad bought Mum that ring back when they had a successful business, but he ruined all of that. The worst thing is, I couldn't find it and didn't have time to search properly."

"What about Marcus?" asked Susie, voice flat, like none of it had sunk in yet.

"What about him? He was a snake too. Deserved the same fate. But I didn't have a way to get him up there, so had to resort to more basic methods."

"You forced him, didn't you?" I said. "The poor man knew you were planning to make him jump."

"He was a gibbering wreck. Weak and pathetic. I had a knife to his side, and took my chance when he ran off like a big baby because his precious dog couldn't get married. Ridiculous. I'd planned to call him and lure the idiot inside the building as I didn't have much time before Amy would be pestering me, but I didn't even need to bother."

"He was a kind man underneath his annoying complaining," said Freya. "He would never have ruined your family business on purpose."

"He would, and he did. Neither of them cared one bit about us, and I pleaded with them both. Up themselves, and full of their own deluded self-importance. That Marcus was a snivelling wreck once I held my knife to him, and he cried as he climbed up the wall. I promised that if he stood on the top I'd let him live, and maybe I would have."

"You're lying, and we know it," said Dad. "You would never have let him back down. He'd go to the police."

"Maybe you're right," laughed Peter. "But it doesn't matter, because I didn't even have to push him. He was up on the wall and shaking so badly that when he lifted his arm to shield his eyes he suddenly fell off. The man was an utter idiot."

"What about the wedding ring? Was that anything to do with you?" I asked.

"I don't know anything about that. I wanted Mum's ring, but if there was a ring where Marcus fell, that's just one of those things."

"He wasn't pushed?" checked Uncle Ernie.

"Mate, that's nasty," said Dubman.

"It's nothing compared to what they both did. They deserved to die. How dare they treat people like that? Now it's done, and I'm not sorry. But if anyone tries to stop me, I'll cut them. I won't hesitate, and I will not go to jail for this." Peter pulled a knife from his cargo pocket and held it firm, his grip tight, hand steady. He sneered at me and growled, "The dog too. I mean it. Don't make me kill the dog."

"I would never risk his life for you." I bent to Anxious and told him, "Stay. No chasing." He looked from me to Peter then back again, but sat and remained quiet.

Peter backed away; nobody moved to stop him.

"Where will you go?" called Amy. "This is dumb. Peter, you need to put the knife away and go to the police. What do you think you can do? You can't go on the run."

"I'll start again somewhere else. I can wait for the heat to die down then begin a new life."

"Don't be daft, son," said Dad. "You won't get far driving an ambulance. Not exactly subtle, is it?"

"No, you're right. What I need is something less obvious. A campervan maybe," he grinned, glaring at me.

My heart actually skipped a beat. I couldn't lose her. Not my Vee. I felt physically sick at the thought of Peter taking Vee away from me, and knew I'd try to stop him, even if it meant risking my life. Or would I? I was in turmoil as Peter approached, waving his blade at the others so they'd back away, but his focus on me.

Anxious remained rooted to the spot. He wasn't going to move aside.

"Anxious, move," I whispered, my words hardly coming out as the reality of the situation hit.

He turned, wagged once, then backed up and sat by my side.

Dad took the other side, and Mum stood next to Anxious.

"You two, move it. Just Max close to me. We're going to go to the car park and Max is going to hand over the keys, and everyone else will get into the dumb wedding planners' van. I want your phones first." Peter grinned at what he believed to be a smart idea, and one by one he took everyone's phones then stuffed them into his jacket pocket.

"Nobody threatens my family," warned Dad as Peter got within striking distance.

"Oh yeah?" he sneered. "What you gonna do about it, old man? You want a taste of this, do you?" Peter thrust out with the knife, a warning to keep his distance, but Dad didn't even flinch.

"How dare you!" snapped Mum, her pale neck flushing.

"Everyone turn around and get in front of Max. Max, you're beside me. If anyone, and I mean anyone, tries to run, or do anything dumb, then Max will get his insides messed up when I stab him. Anyone ever been poked in the kidneys with a knife? No? So don't let it happen because you tried to be clever. Now shift it!"

With little choice, our small group turned, and with Peter keeping the tip of the knife pressed against my side, we made our way slowly towards the car park. Anxious behaved impeccably, keeping pace with us, continually glancing at me and Peter to ensure nothing bad happened, but he didn't try to intervene.

I knew he understood the severity of the situation because not once did his tail wag, and for the little guy, that was unheard of. Anxious' outlook on life was one of utterly unfounded optimism. That at each and every moment of his existence something utterly awesome was most likely going to happen. Be it a cuddle with Sir Snugglington IV, a walk, a treat, a ball to chase, or a stroke of the head, he took joy in every moment of his life, so for him to be serious for this amount of time was shocking.

We passed tourists keen to see the cathedral and the Bishop's Palace before the heat became unbearable, but nobody gave us a second glance as our party weaved along the paths and crossed the grass, until finally we reached the car park.

"Line up by the van," Peter ordered, moving the knife to my belly so nobody was in any doubt about his intentions.

"Don't you dare hurt my boy," growled Mum, giving Peter a glare that should have made him burst into flames, but all he did was stagger.

"Just move it." Once everyone had obeyed, he told Freya, "Open up the back, then get in."

Freya opened the doors, revealing the catering equipment and various items from the previous day's festivities.

"Now hand me the keys, then everyone get inside."

"We won't fit in there," protested Mum, glancing down, clearly worried her dress might get ruined. No matter the circumstances, she was very precious about her clothes.

"You'll fit, or I'll stab Max."

Reluctantly, one by one they crawled into the van, moving boxes and folded tables aside to make enough room. Susie went in first, then Freya, followed by Amy and Rachel. Uncle Ernie smiled weakly at me, then stepped inside. With Mum, Dad, and Dubman still to go, the van was already cramped, but when Dubman shrugged to say that was it, Peter waved the knife at him.

"It's okay," I told Mum. "Don't worry about me. You know I can look after myself, and I have Anxious."

Mum nodded, then told Anxious, "Protect my boy. There's a biscuit in it for you if you do."

Anxious' ears pricked up but his tail remained still. I was beginning to worry he'd lost his wag permanently, which would be disastrous.

Dad went in next, then helped Mum inside, leaving Dubman until last.

"In you go," encouraged Peter, shaking the knife at my side.

Once everyone was inside, and with me nodding to them that everything would be fine, Peter slammed the door shut then locked the van. He took me across the grass to my beautiful VW campervan and ordered me to unlock the side door.

"You get in the back. The dog too. Dog first."

"You're taking us with you?"

"For a while. I might need you. Now get in."

I unlocked the side door, opened it wide, asked Anxious to get in, then took a step up. With my plan formulated, I acted, and feigned a trip. As I fell forward, Anxious wagged, and I spun onto my back. With all the force I could muster, I grabbed the tiny table that swung out from behind the passenger seat and shoved it out. It slammed into Peter's stomach, winding him, and as the knife clattered to the ground and he stumbled backwards, I told Anxious, "Jump!"

My heroic best buddy launched onto the table, then sprang out after Peter as he tripped on the curb and crashed onto the grass.

Anxious landed on his chest and snarled before locking his small but undoubtedly deadly jaws onto Peter's neck.

I jumped from the floor of Vee and warned, "You make a single move, and I mean even twitching your finger, and he'll rip your throat out."

As if to prove he could, Anxious growled, the sound worrying even to my ears as the muffled warning caused Peter to stiffen.

Retrieving the knife, I threw it into the van then quickly opened a drawer under the kitchen counter and pulled out a bag of cable ties I found useful for all manner of things, then sat on Peter's legs while I secured his hands. Then I grabbed his legs and secured them too.

"Good job, Anxious. You saved the day," I congratulated.

His tail began to wag, then spun faster and faster. He was back!

"Um, you can let him go now," I suggested.

With a final warning growl, Anxious released his prisoner then turned and sat facing me, tail swishing side to side in Peter's ghost-white face.

I took the keys from his pocket, then we raced over to the van and I opened the doors and released my very hot and sweaty family and friends, much to their delight and relief.

"That's my boy," beamed Dad as he helped Mum out. They both enveloped me in their love, and I wondered if they'd ever let me go.

Only the insistent barking of Anxious saved me from suffocation by adoring parents, so Mum took a handful of biscuits off me and led Anxious aside to make good on her promise.

We raced back over to Peter and stood around watching him squirm on the pavement. He never said another word to any of us, even after I'd retrieved the phones and called the police. Not knowing what else to do, I made everyone a drink and we sat nursing cups of tea outside Vee on the grass.

"Could have been worse," said Mum merrily as she sipped her brew and the sound of sirens grew closer.

"How?" everyone chorused.

"At least my dress didn't get dirty," she said, winking at me. I leaned over and kissed her forehead. "What was that for?" she asked, smiling happily.

"Just to say never change who you are. After all that happened, and you're still so positive. It's astonishing."

"She's an astonishing lady," laughed Dad. "Hey, and now we've got a great drive back home with the motorbike and sidecar. Turned out alright in the end."

"I am not going anywhere in that deathtrap ever again! I already told you that."

They continued bickering while I sipped my tea and patted my wagging dog.

Chapter 20

"Hey, Max."

"Hey."

Uncle Ernie settled into the chair beside me and sighed as he removed his hat and rubbed at his buzzcut. Unusually for him, he was wearing shorts, black and tight to match his Fred Perry shirt and white braces, and as my eyes tracked down from his skinny legs to his feet, I gasped.

"White Crocs? I don't think I've ever seen you out of black shoes in my life."

"Thought I'd try something different. You inspired me. I popped to the shops this afternoon because I wanted to let the girls spend time together."

"How are they?"

"Bewildered, is the best I can describe it. Too much has happened, and I don't think any of us have taken it all in yet. At least I can say my wedding was memorable," he chuckled, replacing his hat.

"It certainly was. How's Susie holding up?"

"Better than expected. I think she's relieved more than anything. Not that Neil's dead, but that he's gone from her life. And especially now the killer's been found. She's so grateful. We all are."

"That's good she's handling it. What about Freya and Rachel? Are they going to make it as friends?"

"I'm sure they will. I know I shouldn't lie to my wife, and this isn't exactly lying, but let's keep what Rachel did between us."

"So you're certain she messed with the cakes?"

"I had a word with her and she admitted it. She was so sorry, and apologised, and even said she'd own up. I told her not to, as they go back a long way and poor Rachel just got overcome with jealousy and concern about losing her best friend. Let's keep it that way."

"Sure. Whatever you want. Rachel's a good woman, and I understand why she did it. Not that it excuses her behaviour, but I promise I won't say a word."

"Max, let me ask you a question."

"Go ahead." I wiggled my feet in the grass, enjoying the relative cool under the sun shelter, and waited for Uncle Ernie to ask what I knew he would.

After a moment to gather his thoughts, he asked, "How'd you know it was Peter? I was certain it was one of the guests, and had my eye on Rachel, especially after what happened on the beach with the cake. I was going to accuse her before you explained who you believed it was. Why him?"

"I know it sounds daft, but it was the crisps. For a while, when we spotted Amy at the shop with her snacks, I thought it was her, but then I got to thinking about what was found up on the parapet, and she wasn't eating cheese and onion. She told me she had a thing for salt and vinegar crisps and nothing else. Peter loved cheese and onion according to Amy, and then I figured out the rest."

"But how did you work it out? You didn't know about his mum until you spoke with Amy, did you?"

"No, but once I did, I put two and two together. Neil and Marcus were so full of themselves, and Susie herself said that they'd put numerous people out of business because they loved to catch any mistakes with their books, and when Amy explained about Peter's mum and I recalled the way he acted when he first saw Marcus' body, and how they were so close by, everything clicked into place."

"You're a smart guy, Max, and we can't thank you enough."

"It was no big deal," I shrugged.

"Are you mad? Of course it was. Everyone else said it was suicide, but you listened to us and followed through. Even the police dismissed what we said, but not you. You did great."

"Cheers. One thing I wasn't right about was the other ring though. I figured they had to be linked, but they weren't."

"Sometimes there are just coincidences."

"Yes, but at least finding the two led me down the right path. I feel bad for Peter in a way, as he clearly became unhinged over the years the more he stewed on what happened. Imagine going through life like that."

"Poor lad," agreed Uncle Ernie. "But that doesn't excuse what he did. It was a terrible thing, and he'll be punished for it. Right, I've got things to do, so best be off. I just wanted to come and say thank you again." Uncle Ernie stood, Anxious crawled out from under Vee, seemingly having been oblivious to his arrival, then wagged as he had a fuss.

"We'll walk to the gate with you to stretch our legs. I'll fall asleep otherwise."

"You deserve a nap, but sure."

Together, the three of us wandered up the track then we said our goodbyes.

Feeling good about things, as at least now Susie understood what happened and could move on with her life, although I hoped their business was still viable, I strolled back to my pitch leisurely, enjoying the quiet.

As we approached the van, the air seemed to change, and Anxious' hackles rose before he raced off, barking. I hurried after him, the tingle at the back of my neck growing stronger. Anxious sped past our pitch and down the track, going crazy, so I charged after him. A moment later he returned, panting, looking confused. We searched the various paths, but encountered nothing but tents and tourists, so eventually gave up the chase and walked cautiously back up the incline to Vee.

I dreaded what I would find, and it turned out to be for good reason.

On the seat of my chair was a familiar brown envelope. I unwound the string fastener, lifted the flap, and peered inside. Confused by what I discovered, I upended the contents into my palm.

"Teeth? Why teeth?" I wondered.

There was no note this time, just a handful of teeth including molars and incisors from an adult. I carefully returned them to the envelope, fastened it up, then entered Vee and opened the drawer now home to a worrying number of threats. I had the pestle and mortar, the knife, the notes with various warnings, and since yesterday I'd added envelopes containing sand and washed glass, plus now I had teeth. With warnings ranging from the stalker saying my time would come, and he knew what I did, I was still none the wiser about what any of this was about.

Why could I solve so many mysteries, but when it came to personal threats I seemed incapable of figuring it out? I had to get to the bottom of this, and soon, because I was truly rattled and felt like I was being watched constantly.

But for now, there was nothing to do apart from sit in my chair and decide what to make for my dinner. Having foregone a one-pot wonder yesterday, I decided to make up for it today and cook something incredible.

Lost to daydreams of bubbling pots and eating lots, I drifted off to sleep feeling content with my lot, but there was a definite edge to my vanlife now. I vowed to do everything in my power to ensure that my happy existence continued.

When I woke up, I was humming a familiar tune, and the urge to buy a Fudge became too much to resist.

The End

Except it isn't. Read on for a wonderful recipe perfect for a warm summer's evening, and a little more about the next book in the series. With a name like Ninjas and Nightmares, I hope I've managed to pique your interest!

First, let's cook.

Recipe

Barbecue Mackerel

This might not be exactly one-pot cooking, although you could certainly cook it in a Dutch Oven if you wished, but seeing as how Max went to all the "effort" (sorry, couldn't resist!) of catching and cooking the fish, I figured we should take a closer look at exactly how he did it.

The most important thing here is fish that is super fresh; today's catch if at all possible.

You may believe the following recipe to be almost too simple, but sometimes you have to let the star of the show shine as brightly as possible—it's the only way to do it justice. If you try this, I can guarantee you will not be disappointed with either the taste or the lack of washing up!

Ingredients

- 4 whole mackerel, scaled and gutted (heads removed if you like)
- Olive oil - 2 tbsp
- Garlic - 2 cloves crushed
- Lemons - 2 sliced
- Red chilli - one finely chopped
- Coriander - a small bunch chopped, stalks only
- Fennel seeds - 1 tsp
- Salt and pepper to taste

Method

This is great on the barbecue, but perfectly lovely done in the oven too.

- Slash each mackerel a few times on each side and then place in a large roasting tray and top with a drizzle of olive oil.
- In a small bowl, mix the garlic, sliced lemon, chilli, coriander stalks, fennel seeds, and salt and pepper with the olive oil.
- Place the sliced lemon in the fish cavities and rub the rest of the mixture over the fish. Give it a good rub to make sure the flavours can really get into the flesh (including in the slashes you made earlier).
- Add the whole tray to a hot oven (220C/425F) for 10-15 mins or pop each fish onto the grill of a pre-heated barbecue and cook for 3-5 minutes a side. The fish is cooked when it will flake away from the bone easily.
- Done. Bon appétit!

You will probably want something to go alongside the fish. I'd go a simple green salad of rocket and watercress with a zesty dressing. For some carby goodness we'll serve this with some cooled white basmati rice into which we've stirred some lime juice, chopped sweet peppers, the chopped coriander leaves, and another diced chilli.

Perfect summer beach barbecue vibes! Very simple but very tasty too. A good excuse to get the rods out?

From the Author

Max is getting stressed, and that's not good for our hero. Next thing you know, he'll be forgetting to have a pocketful of biscuits at all times, and what will Anxious do without his treats?

Let's hope the gang manage to uncover who's threatening their way of life, and soon. That's not all though. The next book sees the return of a favourite sidekick, and some truly astonishing events lead our vanlifer into one nightmare after another, but always with a few laughs along the way. Grab a copy of Ninjas and Nightmares, but beware, as this time there are frights aplenty!

Be sure to stay updated about new releases and fan sales. You'll hear about them first. No spam, just book updates at www.authortylerrhodes.com.

You can also follow me on Amazon www.amazon.com/stores/author/B0BN6T2VQ5.

Connect with me on Facebook www.facebook.com/authortylerrhodes/

Printed in Great Britain
by Amazon